Poet to Poet
Wordsworth Selected by Lawrence Durrell

William Wordsworth, poet and critic, was born in
Cumberland in 1770. He went to Cambridge in 1787
and later in 1790 to France, attracted by the French
Revolution. He and Coleridge published *Lyrical Ballads*,
which included 'Tintern Abbey' in 1789. *The Prelude* is
considered Wordsworth's masterpiece. He became Poet
Laureate in 1843 and died in 1850

Lawrence Durrell, poet and novelist, was born of
British parents in India in 1912. His *Collected Poems*
were published in 1960. Some of his best-known novels
are *The Black Book* (1938), the four novels under the
general title *The Alexandria Quartet* (1957–60), *Tunc*
(1968) and its sequel *Nunquam* (1969).

WORDSWORTH

Selected by

Lawrence Durrell

Penguin Books

Penguin Books Ltd, Harmondsworth,
Middlesex, England
Penguin Books Inc., 7110 Ambassador Road,
Baltimore, Maryland 21207, USA
Penguin Books Australia Ltd,
Ringwood, Victoria, Australia

First published 1973
Selection and Introduction copyright © Lawrence Durrell, 1973

Made and printed in Great Britain by
Richard Clay (The Chaucer Press) Ltd,
Bungay, Suffolk
Set in Monotype Ehrhardt

Contents

Introduction by Lawrence Durrell   9

Written in Very Early Youth   23
To a Butterfly   24
Characteristics of a Child Three Years Old   25
Lucy Gray; or, Solitude   26
Rural Architecture   29
To H.C. Six Years Old   30
Lesbia (Catullus, V)   32
Argument for Suicide   33
She dwelt among the untrodden ways   34
I travelled among unknown men   35
Ere with cold beads of midnight dew   36
To —   37
The Forsaken   38
from Michael   39
Farewell Lines   40
A slumber did my spirit seal   41
Lines Composed a Few Miles above Tintern Abbey   42
French Revolution   47
Dedication. To —   49
Nuns fret not at their convent's narrow room   50
Why, Minstrel, these untuneful murmurings   51
To Sleep   52
To Sleep   53
Surprised by joy – impatient as the Wind   54
It is a beauteous evening, calm and free   55
The world is too much with us; late and soon   56
Retirement   57

Those words were uttered as in pensive mood 58
September, 1815 59
November 1 60
Composed During a Storm 61
Though narrow be that old Man's cares, and near 62
Four fiery steeds impatient of the rein 63
Composed upon Westminster Bridge, September 3, 1802 64
When Philoctetes in the Lemnian isle 65
While Anna's peers and early playmates tread 66
To — 67
The Infant M — M — 68
A Poet! – He hath put his heart to school 69
The most alluring clouds that mount the sky 70
Oh what a Wreck! how changed in mien and speech! 71
In my mind's eye a Temple, like a cloud 72
At Furness Abbey 73
At the Grave of Burns, 1803 74
The Solitary Reaper 77
Composed in the Valley near Dover, on the Day of
    Landing 79
London, 1802 80
Avaunt all specious pliancy of mind 81
The French and the Spanish Guerillas 82
Composed in One of the Catholic Cantons 83
Sky-Prospect – from the Plain of France 84
On Being Stranded near the Harbour of Boulogne 85
At Rome 86
Near the Same Lake 87
The Cuckoo at Laverna 88
At the Convent of Camaldoli 92
Continued 93
Among the Ruins of a Convent in the Apennines 94
Return, Content! for fondly I pursued 95
from The River Duddon: After-thought 96

The pibroch's note, discountenanced or mute   97
Composed in the Glen of Loch Etive   98
Eagles   99
Suggested at Tyndrum in a Storm   100
'Rest and Be Thankful'   101
The Highland Broach   102
Roman Antiquities   105
from The White Doe of Rylstone   106
Crusades   107
Places of Worship   108
Mutability   109
Soft as a cloud is yon blue Ridge – the Mere   110
Desire we past illusions to recal?   111
On Revisiting Dunolly Castle   112
Cave of Staffa   113
Steamboats, Viaducts, and Railways   114
Expostulation and Reply   115
The Tables Turned   117
A Character   119
A Poet's Epitaph   120
Personal Talk   123
Ode to Duty   126
Young England – what is then become of Old   129
Goody Blake and Harry Gill   130
To a Child   135
Hast thou seen, with flash incessant   136
The Old Cumberland Beggar   137
Animal Tranquillity and Decay   144
Invocation to the Earth   145
Ode; Intimations of Immortality from Recollections of
    Early Childhood   147
From the Alfoxden Notebook   155
Written in the Strangers' Book at 'The Station', opposite
    Bowness   156

from The Prelude (*1850 edition*)
    from Book I: Childhood and School-Time,
    lines 357–478 157
    from Book XI: France, lines 105–44;
    lines 206–58 161

from The Excursion
    from Book I: The Wanderer, lines 201–26 164
    from Book V: The Pastor, lines 671–92;
    lines 705–27 165
    from Book VI: The Churchyard among the
    Mountains, lines 212–61 166

Introduction

The problem of Wordsworth the poet has always been be-
devilled by the double image of the man – created, one
supposes, by himself, though it has been suggested that it was
the work of Hartley Coleridge when he observed: 'What a
mighty genius is the poet Wordsworth! What a dull proser is
W. W. Esqre of Rydal Mount, Distributor of Stamps and
brother to the Revnd. The Master of Trinity.' At any rate
Hartley (who had inherited much of his father's vivacity of
mind and bright insight) was the first to set up the double
Wordsworth, and all subsequent critics have accepted the
same point of departure easily enough. It finds its way into
most critical estimates of the poet's work, even today.
Throughout the twenties and thirties the two Wordsworths
were a convenient cockshy for satirists. Was it not Squire? –
it was either he or Shanks who published the following lines
in the *London Mercury*.

> Two voices are there. One is loud and deep,
> And one is of an old half-witted sheep,
> And Wordsworth, both are thine . . .

But it can be made into a persuasive case only by those who
have not been faced (as the present editor has been) with the
sum total of Wordsworth's work to read at one blow – supple-
mented by a comprehensive and sensitive biography of the
man. This procedure is guaranteed to surprise one, for the
case of Wordsworth becomes more intricate and less clear-cut
than it would be convenient to believe; he remained the same
man, operating on all the different levels, completely un-

divided. His political principles were as much part of him as his poetic ones or his religious attitudes and beliefs, and the poetry (the best and the worst) overshadows all these activities, by turn lyrical, didactic, elegaic or hortatory. For the first time one realizes how all-of-a-piece the work is, and how in the back of the poet's own mind, all the parts constituted fragments from a single huge work of autobiographical confession – a depiction of the growth of a poet's mind and sensibility.

It was a tremendously ambitious undertaking just to be Mr William Wordsworth, and to be aware of his vocation and his poetic responsibilities towards it; and it is marvellous to see with what fortitude and in what exemplary degree he managed to discharge them over such a long and truthful life – he died at the age of eighty. Studied in this way he cannot help but grow in stature rather than diminish. Everything – even his less successful work – becomes significant and enriching. Every detail adds, once one sees the character of the man with any clearness.

Wordsworth almost more than any other English poet enjoyed a sense of inner confirmation – the mysterious sense of election to poetry as a whole way of life. He realized too that one cannot condescend to nature – one must work for it like a monk over a missal which he will not live to see finished. He felt he was hunting for what was most itself in nature, the poised and limpid truth of reality. Poetry was his lariat. So that what might, by ignorant or prejudiced critics, be represented as being in some parts the unpolished maunderings of some neurotic sectary, given to introspection, turns out when seen as a whole, as a lifestyle, to which the writing was a mere appendix, a mere illustration: turns out to be one of the most determined, thoughtful, pure and disinterested attempts by any poet since Milton to purge and mature a human intuition by the practice of poetry – using the direct vision of the natural world as both touchstone and lodestar. The furniture of his universe was nature in all its multi-plicity – not a pack of moral attributes or a clique of allegorical figures.

Wordsworth was a man from the craggy north, a blunt man full of psychic obstinacy. He set himself to see nature as a whole, as something more than the sum of its parts. He was celebrating those mysterious 'visitations' of which he speaks – flashes of blinding intuition which gave him glimpses of something like process itself at work . . . There was to be no nonsense about this task, to which he had been called by the deepest part of his own nature. He pitched his work beyond the reach of the contemporary 'poetical' style and made it low-toned, monochrome in tinge. Though in no way a moral-ist, he seems to have felt that if one sought and found Truth one would insensibly find goodness there, for they were part of the same animal. And ultimate goodness came from an intuition which had fulfilled itself in its commerce with mother nature: poetry was simply the outward and visible sign of such a search. The originality and magnitude of such a venture for such a man lay in the fact that it carefully side-stepped a dogmatic theology in an age when it was almost impossible to do so comfortably, particularly for a man of his birth and background, and in the circumstances imposed by the society of his time and place.

Indeed, when one reflects on his life, one is astonished at the pitfalls he managed to escape; his birth was into a back-ground of parsons, dons, prosperous lawyers, mariners. Minor gentry one might say, which is to suggest a certain level of refinement and culture – at the least the possession of books. Wordsworth's father gave him the run of a small but choice library – an inestimable gift for an incipient poet. Yet it was also the age of nonconformity, of republicanism, of transcendentalism. Wordsworth when young was a convinced republican, and like every other warm-hearted intelligence welcomed the French Revolution without reserve. But his idealism was bitterly disappointed, almost to the point of trauma, by the excesses he witnessed during his French residence and his subsequent loathing and fear of republicanism seems to date from his return. Ironically enough he also fell in love with a French girl (a Royalist in politics) by whom he had an illegitimate daughter. Separated by war for many years, he finally decided against marriage to her, but he never wavered as far as his responsibilities were concerned towards the daughter. He acknowledged his paternity, and later sent her money, and visited her on the most affectionate and friendly basis. But his own real interior poetic life unfolded itself when at last he was free to set up house with his beloved sister Dorothy – a dream they had cherished for a long time, and in which she took her natural place as the poet's real Muse. Later he married an old family friend, and collected quite a little harem of eager and affectionate copyists for his work – the 'family of Love', as someone called it, impressed by the dignity and harmony of their communal life.

Naturally the psychoanalysts have made Wordsworth, like so many other creative men, a stalking-horse for their theories. I am personally sympathetic to Freud's views and believe that Wordsworth himself would have been fascinated by them. But surely it was Freud who once wrote: 'Before the mystery of the creative act psychoanalysis lays down its arms'? Yet there is no need for an exaggerated display of clinical tact in this case, if 'case' it be, for what is resolved during an analysis of a neurosis is precisely the same sort of tension which is resolved in the act of creation by a major poet. He makes, so to speak, models of his anxieties, and fits them into his life-constellation, submitting himself to the stresses and strains of

the business, often risking ill-health or even madness in order
to affront and tame them. (St George and the Dragon.) The
poetic work, in interpreting these terrors through art, helps
him to surmount them in his life. ('The great masters', writes
Proust, 'are those who master themselves.') Indeed the life-
work of a great poet – a Valéry, Rilke, Yeats – should be
considered as a long process of triumphantly surmounting his
anxieties, his complexes, the wounds which his infantile
psyche bears, by the act of exteriorizing them, of giving them
form. We, his readers, profit vicariously from the transaction
of reading and studying such work, for it helps us to do the
same with our own stresses. (Each poem is a cry of relief, of
victory over the hippogriff.) In the case of William Words-
worth, his work might well be likened to the long and horrible
self-analysis undertaken by Freud at the beginning of his
career as a healer, an operation nobody else was capable of
performing for him. 'Each original work of art', cries Words-
worth, 'must create the taste by which it is to be judged.'
Read and mark!

Of course his beloved sister Dorothy took the place of his
dead mother and in the voluptuousness of the transference he
was able to feel the comfort and reassurance of his early
childhood repeat itself in manhood. Moreover she was no
dried-up old maid but a marvellous devoted woman who was
the perfect partner in life; in every way sapient enough,
intelligent enough, to second his growth. Most of all, it was
she who set an exact value on his work, convincing him that it
was worth living for and worth starving for. Very well, you
may say, it was a surrogate-reassurance to replace what he had
lost. But all the more lucky for us that so sensitive and reticent
a poet should have such a sister, who demanded nothing of
him except love and poetry, and for her part readily supplied
the sympathy and the hard work necessary to keep the whole
household oriented towards him. It was love all right, but it

was a love of a marvellous self-abnegation – the love of Héloïse and Abelard, one might say. So at least says the poet himself in more than one place. It outstripped all thought of real sexuality. (How astonished the brother and sister would be to read this last paragraph!)

> Then it was
> That the beloved Woman in whose sight
> Those days were pass'd, now speaking in a voice
> Of sudden admonition, like a brook
> That did but cross a lonely road, and now
> Seen, heard and felt, and caught at every turn,
> Companion never lost through many a league,
> Maintained for me a saving intercourse
> With my true self; for, though impair'd and chang'd
> Much, as it seem'd, I was no further chang'd
> Than as a clouded, not a waning moon:
> She, in the midst of all, preserv'd me still
> A Poet, made me seek beneath that name
> My office upon earth, and nowhere else.

Looked at from this point of view the famous lines written above Tintern Abbey could be considered one of the great love-poems in the language.

The traditional portrait of the poet is drawn for the most part from the synoptic view of his life which tells us, for example, that the revolutionary young man spent 1791–2 in France, watched the first excesses of the revolution, fell in love with Annette Vallon who bore him a daughter, and then returned to England with his head hung low and his revolutionary heart broken by what he regarded not simply as an internal French disaster, but as a betrayal of the hopes for the whole human race. He was not the only one – a whole generation of young freethinkers and utopians all over Europe felt the same. A sick disgust, a heart-wrenching disappointment.

Moreover this dark experience mingled with his despair about his French lover; he had every intention of marrying her and bringing her back to England – all this to the delight of Dorothy who at once established friendly and indeed loving contact with the girl. But a mixture of circumstances both personal and international intervened and separated them, not least among them the war with Napoleon, and gradually the marriage prospects faded out of the picture.

Nevertheless, so honest was Wordsworth, that when he fell in love with someone else he insisted on clearing the matter with Annette. In everything we have to deal with a highly collected man and a high-principled one. He was master of his own ship, however much his infantile poet-side quailed before life and drew strength from the women about him. War put the finishing touches to his French love affair, and he turned away towards his English destiny, with perhaps many regrets and certainly some unjustified self-reproach. It is from this point onward that his life seems to become staider, more orthodox, less colourful. He had been disappointed both in love and in his political visions of human justice. There remained his art. It is worth remembering that later on he married an old family friend, and that for a long time, while he lived with his sister, they took joint charge of a small child which belonged to a widower friend in London who could not meet his responsibilities towards the infant. In other words the household structure was a real one, a homelike one in the real sense of the word. It did not lack a domestic shape capable of engendering for the Wordsworths real human contact, warmth and responsibility. Moreover they were all happily devotees of country life, and adepts at facing the rigours of climate and the boredom of long winters in the north. To them their native landscape was a Paradise, an Eden, and they never, like other Romantics, hankered for Italy or Greece. Switzerland represented something more real for Wordsworth, not only because it was scenically grandiose but also because it embodied the highest expression of democratic values. When Napoleon invaded it Wordsworth became his implacable enemy, and his sonnets were clarion-calls to rouse the English to their responsibilities towards the rights of man and the freedom of states – and the defeat of tyrants. As time went on Wordsworth may be represented as shifting his allegiances from republicanism to high toryism; was this the inevitable hardening of the arteries which comes after forty or was it based on a measured view of man and his capacities – his ability to deal rationally and sensibly with freedom? I like to presume the latter, though the evidence goes against me. One wonders where he would stand today amidst so many conflicting issues? One is reminded of a jotting by the indefatigable Crabb Robinson:

Wordsworth spoke with great feeling of the present state of the country. He considers the combinations among journeymen, and even the Benefit Societies and all associations of men, apparently for the best purposes, as very alarming: he contemplates the renovation of all the horrors of a war between the poor and the rich, a conflict of property with no property.

The memories of the French terror, and the reign of Robespierre, had left their mark.

Young De Quincey has noted somewhere the rate of growth of Wordsworth's reputation. 'Up to 1820,' he writes, 'the name of Wordsworth was trampled underfoot; from 1820 to 1830 it was militant; from 1830 to 1835 it has been triumphant.' There is something almost irresistible in the steady deliberate advance of the poet, not simply upon his public, but upon the sentiment of the whole nation. He gradually expanded into a grave public figure, a symbol of the vigour and maturity of English literature. Perhaps even a graven image to some, or a sacred cow. To continue the story, in 1839 Oxford honoured him with a D.C.L. In 1842 he was accorded a civil list pension which enabled him to resign his sinecure as a Distributor of Stamps which he had held, discharging his duties aptly and faithfully, since 1813. He succeeded, finally, Southey as Poet Laureate in 1843. In 1850, at the ripe age of eighty, Wordsworth died. He was the father of five children, and his wife lived on for another nine years after his death. His renown was nation-wide.

Side by side with his poetic life Wordsworth lived a fruitful and purposeful private life of a family man, passed for the most part in the most quiet and beautiful part of the one countryside which he loved above all others and to which he belonged. In many ways, if one adds up the debit and credit, he was almost supernaturally lucky. To live, first of all, exactly where he wished to; then to devote his whole time, his whole spirit, to his vocation. Poetry was both his life and his *business*. There were moments of hesitation when during his youth he was threatened with having to take a job – becoming a parson or a tutor – and then he felt his poetic independence threatened. But each time the clouds passed and the future allowed him to set his feet upon the path to selfhood, and with it to fame. Has there ever been a poet (without a private income) half as lucky as he? And then, Dorothy Wordsworth – what a gift from the Gods this sister turned out to be. Her invincible devotion to him – and not only to him, but to his work – made a shelter in which his mind could take refuge. The little harem of copyists existed only to further his aims, to make life easy for him. With such an ambience it would have been impossible not to make the best of one's art. No wonder Wordsworth did his work entirely without the use of drugs, or even the abuse of alcohol. He was perhaps the only poet of his age to manage to work thus. Of course so sensitive a man could not expect to be free from the strains and stresses of creative unhappiness – he would have been exceptional indeed had he never shown a sign of distress or anxiety. One remembers the pain in his side which often prevented him working, and which he outfaced; one remembers the eye-trouble; and also the periods of nervous stress which gave the attentive Dorothy so much cause for alarm and misgiving. But in the end it was Dorothy and not William who suffered a mental overthrow.

Yes, there were occasional money troubles too, and the need to secure himself a sinecure from the distribution of stamps arose in middle life. But this involved only local travelling. He was never forced to leave his own countryside. He always found admirers to let him rent or borrow congenial places to live with his family. Moreover his calculated frugality put him beyond the scope of those to whom he might have found himself indebted had he been a borrower or a spendthrift. If his luck was good, his credit was also, and in money matters he showed conspicuous good sense.

The existence of a definitive text of the poetry, and of more than one comprehensive biography of the poet, gives one the courage if not the right to pick about in the record of his long life in order to isolate if possible the high spots and the low, the miracles of good luck and the calamities which beset him – no poet can hope to sidestep Nemesis entirely; and Wordsworth the family man, the husband and father, had many sorrows to contend with on his line of march. They temper the rather austere after-image he has left us, and point to a man capable of deep passionate feeling underneath his proud reticence – and most of all where his children were concerned.

I am thinking most particularly of the year 1812 which was a particularly bitter one for the Wordsworth family, for two of the small children died during the course of it – little four-year old Catherine first, and then Tom some six months later. Wordsworth's own grief transmuted itself into one of his loveliest poems for the child, though it was not published until much later.

> Surprised by joy – impatient as the Wind
> I turned to share the transport – Oh! with whom
> But Thee, deep buried in the silent tomb,
> That spot which no vicissitude can find?
> Love, faithful love, recalled thee to my mind –

But there were other bitternesses almost as hard to surmount, such as the unexpected loss of his adored brother John the sea captain, who went down with the wreck of his ship. This cruel calamity cast a shadow over the hearts of William and Dorothy, for John had been closest to them, and was planning to come one day and share their lives.

Dorothy's own gradual collapse and the gradual foundering of her reason must also have weighed on him a great deal – she was so much his alter ego that it must have seemed like the loss of half of his own mind to watch her slowly descending the long slopes of unreason, to end up as a total mental wreck. All these tragedies he faced with fierce pride and responsibility. Perhaps there were others of which we know nothing, but if his later poetry is coloured by an ever deepening melancholy, a deep gathering pessimism, we might suspect that it was not only due to a gradual loss of faith in man's ability to restore to himself the shattered Paradise which had once seemed (to Wordsworth) within his reach; these private blows of fate must also have helped to charge his poetry with an autumnal sadness, a resignation, perhaps the vibration of his own approaching death. And then the death of his elder married daughter Dora was the final twist of the knife.

Two meetings of a professional kind might be accounted as of capital importance to Wordsworth's thinking. The most important is of course his encounter with the greatest thinker of the age, Coleridge – that unselfish, wayward, haphazard and eccentric genius who rushed into Wordsworth's life like a whirlwind. Never could the poet have hoped for so profound an understanding of his work; but Coleridge brought even more than sympathetic appreciation. He approved the basic principles upon which Wordsworth had founded his poetic style. How moving is this great encounter; and how tragic that this literary friendship (which gave us the *Lyrical Ballads*) was clouded for so long by a silly misunderstanding which both men were big enough to have surmounted. Never mind. Their association fecundated a whole period of our literature.

To this momentous friendship I would add another meeting, perhaps of less consequence in terms of friendship, but of great importance to the poet's intellectual make-up – the meeting with Hamilton, the Irish mathematical genius. Through him Wordsworth learned all that was to be known about modern science – though of course he was getting on in years while Hamilton was still a young man. But he had always had an aptitude for, a fondness for, mathematics.

Another point is worth mentioning. In spite of the somewhat static picture his life gives, Wordsworth's mind was always open to Europe through its aptitudes. By education he was a classicist and humanist, but he also adventured in Italian and German as well as French. He also travelled in Europe increasingly after the wars subsided and the frontiers opened for travellers. His sympathies were generous and universal even if sometimes hidden under a dry and restrained exterior.

The reader should also bear in mind that this poet composed aloud, testing out his verses on the ear, not only on the eye. To do him justice he should be tested on the inner ear, or frankly, aloud. It will serve no purpose to hint at a certain metrical lack of variety in his work, and perhaps a touch of humourlessness. People of this calibre must be judged by their best qualities, and Wordsworth is no exception as he steers his verse around the rocks and shoals which lay in wait for it – over-meekness, sententiousness, too much austerity, too great a rectitude – towards the open sea of English poetry. He knew full well that the reality he sought lay beyond life, and that life was a very fragile and provisional matter.

The poem is an act of affirmation – one dares to make such a statement feeling that Wordsworth would have quietly agreed.

LAWRENCE DURRELL

Written in Very Early Youth

Calm is all nature as a resting wheel.
The kine are couched upon the dewy grass;
The horse alone, seen dimly as I pass,
Is cropping audibly his later meal:
Dark is the ground; a slumber seems to steal
O'er vale, and mountain, and the starless sky.
Now, in this blank of things, a harmony,
Home-felt, and home-created, comes to heal
That grief for which the senses still supply
Fresh food; for only then, when memory
Is hushed, am I at rest. My Friends! restrain
Those busy cares that would allay my pain;
Oh! leave me to myself, nor let me feel
The officious touch that makes me droop again.

To a Butterfly

Stay near me – do not take thy flight!
A little longer stay in sight!
Much converse do I find in thee,
Historian of my infancy!
Float near me; do not yet depart!
Dead times revive in thee:
Thou bring'st, gay creature as thou art!
A solemn image to my heart,
My father's family!

Oh! pleasant, pleasant were the days,
The time, when, in our childish plays,
My sister Emmeline and I
Together chased the butterfly!
A very hunter did I rush
Upon the prey: – with leaps and springs
I followed on from brake to bush;
But she, God love her! feared to brush
The dust from off its wings.

Characteristics of
a Child Three Years Old

Loving she is, and tractable, though wild;
And Innocence hath privilege in her
To dignify arch looks and laughing eyes;
And feats of cunning; and the pretty round
Of trespasses, affected to provoke
Mock-chastisement and partnership in play.
And, as a faggot sparkles on the hearth,
Not less if unattended and alone
Than when both young and old sit gathered round
And take delight in its activity;
Even so this happy Creature of herself
Is all-sufficient; solitide to her
Is blithe society, who fills the air
With gladness and involuntary songs.
Light are her sallies as the tripping fawn's
Forth-startled from the fern where she lay couched;
Unthought-of, unexpected, as the stir
Of the soft breeze ruffling the meadow-flowers,
Or from before it chasing wantonly
The many-coloured images imprest
Upon the bosom of a placid lake.

Lucy Gray;

OR, SOLITUDE

Oft I had heard of Lucy Gray:
And, when I crossed the wild,
I chanced to see at break of day
The solitary child.

No mate, no comrade Lucy knew;
She dwelt on a wide moor,
–The sweetest thing that ever grew
Beside a human door!

You yet may spy the fawn at play,
The hare upon the green;
But the sweet face of Lucy Gray
Will never more be seen.

'To-night will be a stormy night –
You to the town must go;
And take a lantern, Child, to light
You mother through the snow.'

'That, Father! will I gladly do:
'Tis scarcely afternoon –
The minster-clock has just struck two,
And yonder is the moon!'

At this the Father raised his hook,
And snapped a faggot-band;
He plied his work; – and Lucy took
The lantern in her hand.

Not blither is the mountain roe:
With many a wanton stroke
Her feet disperse the powdery snow,
That rises up like smoke.

The storm came on before its time:
She wandered up and down;
And many a hill did Lucy climb:
But never reached the town.

The wretched parents all that night
Went shouting far and wide;
But there was neither sound nor sight
To serve them for a guide.

At day-break on a hill they stood
That overlooked the moor;
And thence they saw the bridge of wood,
A furlong from their door.

They wept – and, turning homeward, cried,
'In heaven we all shall meet;'
– When in the snow the mother spied
The print of Lucy's feet.

Then downwards from the steep hill's edge
They tracked the footmarks small;
And through the broken hawthorn hedge,
And by the long stone-wall;

And then an open field they crossed:
The marks were still the same;
They tracked them on, nor ever lost;
And to the bridge they came.

They followed from the snowy bank
Those footmarks, one by one,
Into the middle of the plank;
And further there were none!

– Yet some maintain that to this day
She is a living child;
That you may see sweet Lucy Gray
Upon the lonesome wild.

O'er rough and smooth she trips along,
And never looks behind;
And sings a solitary song
That whistles in the wind.

Rural Architecture

There's George Fisher, Charles Fleming, and Reginald
    Shore,
Three rosy-cheeked school-boys, the highest not more
Than the height of a counsellor's bag;
To the top of GREAT HOW did it please them to climb:
And there they built up, without mortar or lime,
A Man on the peak of the crag.

They built him of stones gathered up as they lay:
They built him and christened him all in one day,
An urchin both vigorous and hale;
And so without scruple they called him Ralph Jones.
Now Ralph is renowned for the length of his bones;
The Magog of Legberthwaite dale.

Just half a week after, the wind sallied forth,
And in anger or merriment, out of the north,
Coming on with a terrible pother,
From the peak of the crag blew the giant away.
And what did these school-boys? – The very next day
They went and they built up another.

– Some little I've seen of blind boisterous works
By Christian disturbers more savage than Turks,
Spirits busy to do and undo:
At remembrance whereof my blood sometimes will flag;
Then, light-hearted Boys, to the top of the crag;
And I'll build up a giant with you.

To H.C.

O thou! whose fancies from afar are brought;
Who of thy words dost make a mock apparel,
And fittest to unutterable thought
The breeze-like motion and the self-born carol;
Thou faery voyager! that dost float
In such clear water, that thy boat
May rather seem
To brood on air than on an earthly stream;
Suspended in a stream as clear as sky,
Where earth and heaven do make one imagery;
O blessed vision! happy child!
Thou art so exquisitely wild,
I think of thee with many fears
For what may be thy lot in future years.

I thought of times when Pain might be thy guest,
Lord of thy house and hospitality;
And Grief, uneasy lover! never rest
But when she sate within the touch of thee.
O too industrious folly!
O vain and causeless melancholy!
Nature will either end thee quite;
Or, lengthening out thy season of delight,
Preserve for thee, by individual right,
A young lamb's heart among the full-grown flocks.
What hast thou to do with sorrow,
Or the injuries of to-morrow?
Thou art a dew-drop, which the morn brings forth,
Ill fitted to sustain unkindly shocks,

Or to be trailed along the soiling earth;
A gem that glitters while it lives,
And no forewarning gives;
But, at the touch of wrong, without a strife
Slips in a moment out of life.

Lesbia

(Catullus, V)

My Lesbia let us love and live,
And to the winds my Lesbia give
Each cold restraint, each boding fear
Of Age and all her saws severe.
Yon sun now posting to the main
Will set – but 'tis to rise again;
But we, when once our [   ] light
Is set, must sleep in endless night.
Then come, with whom alone I live,
A thousand kisses take and give,
Another thousand – to the store
Add hundreds – then a thousand more,
And when they to a million mount
Let Confusion take the account,
That you, the number never knowing,
May continue still bestowing,
That I for joys may never pine
That never can again be mine.

Argument for Suicide

Send this man to the mine, this to the battle,
Famish an aged beggar at your gates,
And let him die by inches – but for worlds
Lift not your hand against him – Live, live on,
As if this earth owned neither steel nor arsenic,
A rope, a river, or a standing pool.
Live, if you dread the pains of hell, or think
Your corpse would quarrel with a stake – alas
Has misery then no friend? – if you would die
By license, call the dropsy and the stone
And let them end you – strange it is;
And most fantastic are the magic circles
Drawn round the thing called life – till we have learned
To prize it less, we ne'er shall learn to prize
The things worth living for. –

She dwelt among the untrodden ways

She dwelt among the untrodden ways
   Beside the springs of Dove,
A Maid whom there were none to praise
   And very few to love:

A violet by a mossy stone
   Half hidden from the eye!
– Fair as a star, when only one
   Is shining in the sky.

She lived unknown, and few could know
   When Lucy ceased to be;
But she is in her grave, and, oh,
   The difference to me!

I travelled among
unknown men

I travelled among unknown men,
   In lands beyond the sea;
Nor, England! did I know till then
   What love I bore to thee.

'Tis past, that melancholy dream!
   Nor will I quit thy shore
A second time; for still I seem
   To love thee more and more.

Among thy mountains did I feel
   The joy of my desire;
And she I cherished turned her wheel
   Beside an English fire.

Thy mornings showed, thy nights concealed,
   The bowers where Lucy played;
And thine too is the last green field
   That Lucy's eyes surveyed.

Ere with cold beads of midnight dew

Ere with cold beads of midnight dew
   Had mingled tears of thine,
I grieved, fond Youth! that thou shouldst sue
   To haughty Geraldine.

Immoveable by generous sighs,
   She glories in a train
Who drag, beneath our native skies,
   An oriental chain.

Pine not like them with arms across,
   Forgetting in thy care
How the fast-rooted trees can toss
   Their branches in mid air.

The humblest rivulet will take
   Its own wild liberties;
And, every day, the imprisoned lake
   Is flowing in the breeze.

Then crouch no more on suppliant knee,
   But scorn with scorn outbrave;
A Briton, even in love, should be
   A subject, not a slave!

To —

Look at the fate of summer flowers,
Which blow at daybreak, droop ere even-song;
And, grieved for their brief date, confess that ours,
Measured by what we are and ought to be,
Measured by all that, trembling, we foresee,
　　Is not so long!

If human Life do pass away,
Perishing yet more swiftly than the flower,
If we are creatures of a *winter's* day;
What space hath Virgin's beauty to disclose
Her sweets, and triumph o'er the breathing rose?
　　Not even an hour!

The deepest grove whose foliage hid
The happiest lovers Arcady might boast,
Could not the entrance of this thought forbid:
O be thou wise as they, soul-gifted Maid!
Nor rate too high what must so quickly fade,
　　So soon be lost.

Then shall love teach some virtuous Youth
'To draw, out of the object of his eyes,'
The while on thee they gaze in simple truth,
Hues more exalted, 'a refinèd Form,'
That dreads not age, nor suffers from the worm,
　　And never dies.

The Forsaken

The peace which others seek they find;
The heaviest storms not longest last;
Heaven grants even to the guiltiest mind
An amnesty for what is past;
When will my sentence be reversed?
I only pray to know the worst;
And wish, as if my heart would burst.

O weary struggle! silent years
Tell seemingly no doubtful tale;
And yet they leave it short, and fears
And hopes are strong and will prevail.
My calmest faith escapes not pain;
And, feeling that the hope is vain,
I think that he will come again.

from Michael

... No habitation can be seen; but they
Who journey thither find themselves alone
With a few sheep, with rocks and stones, and kites
That overhead are sailing in the sky.
It is in truth an utter solitude;
Nor should I have made mention of this Dell
But for one object which you might pass by,
Might see and notice not. Beside the brook
Appears a straggling heap of unhewn stones!
And to that simple object appertains
A story – unenriched with strange events,
Yet not unfit, I deem, for the fireside,
Or for the summer shade. It was the first
Of those domestic tales that spake to me
Of Shepherds, dwellers in the valleys, men
Whom I already loved; – not verily
For their own sakes, but for the fields and hills
Where was their occupation and abode.
And hence this Tale, while I was yet a Boy
Careless of books, yet having felt the power
Of Nature, by the gentle agency
Of natural objects, led me on to feel
For passions that were not my own, and think
(At random and imperfectly indeed)
On man, the heart of man, and human life.
Therefore, although it be a history
Homely and rude, I will relate the same
For the delight of a few natural hearts;
And, with yet fonder feeling, for the sake
Of youthful Poets, who among these hills
Will be my second self when I am gone ...

Farewell Lines

'High bliss is only for a higher state',
But, surely, if severe afflictions borne
With patience merit the reward of peace,
Peace ye deserve; and may the solid good,
Sought by a wise though late exchange, and here
With bounteous hand beneath a cottage-roof
To you accorded, never be withdrawn,
Nor for the world's best promises renounced.
Most soothing was it for a welcome Friend,
Fresh from the crowded city, to behold
That lonely union, privacy so deep,
Such calm employments, such entire content.
So when the rain is over, the storm laid,
A pair of herons oft-times have I seen,
Upon a rocky islet, side by side,
Drying their feathers in the sun, at ease;
And so, when night with grateful gloom had fallen,
Two glow-worms in such nearness that they shared,
As seemed, their soft self-satisfying light,
Each with the other, on the dewy ground,
Where He that made them blesses their repose. –
When wandering among lakes and hills I note,
Once more, those creatures thus by nature paired,
And guarded in their tranquil state of life,
Even, as your happy presence to my mind
Their union brought, will they repay the debt,
And send a thankful spirit back to you,
With hope that we, dear Friends! shall meet again.

A slumber did my spirit seal

A slumber did my spirit seal;
   I had no human fears:
She seemed a thing that could not feel
   The touch of earthly years.

No motion has she now, no force;
   She neither hears nor sees;
Rolled round in earth's diurnal course,
   With rocks, and stones, and trees.

Lines

COMPOSED A FEW MILES ABOVE TINTERN ABBEY,
ON REVISITING THE BANKS OF THE WYE
DURING A TOUR. JULY 13, 1798

Five years have past; five summers, with the length
of five long winters! and again I hear
These waters, rolling from their mountain-springs
With a soft inland murmur. – Once again
Do I behold these steep and lofty cliffs,
That on a wild secluded scene impress
Thoughts of more deep seclusion; and connect
The landscape with the quiet of the sky.
The day is come when I again repose
Here, under this dark sycamore, and view
These plots of cottage-ground, these orchard-tufts,
Which at this season, with their unripe fruits,
Are clad in one green hue, and lose themselves
'Mid groves and copses. Once again I see
These hedge-rows, hardly hedge-rows, little lines
Of sportive wood run wild: these pastoral farms,
Green to the very door; and wreaths of smoke
Sent up, in silence, from among the trees!
With some uncertain notice, as might seem
Of vagrant dwellers in the houseless woods,
Or of some Hermit's cave, where by his fire
The Hermit sits alone.

                   These beauteous forms,
Through a long absence, have not been to me
As is a landscape to a blind man's eye:
But oft, in lonely rooms, and 'mid the din
Of towns and cities, I have owed to them

In hours of weariness, sensations sweet,
Felt in the blood, and felt along the heart;
And passing even into my purer mind,
With tranquil restoration: – feelings too
Of unremembered pleasure: such, perhaps,
As have no slight or trivial influence
On that best portion of a good man's life,
His little, nameless, unremembered, acts
Of kindness and of love. Nor less, I trust,
To them I may have owed another gift,
Of aspect more sublime; that blessed mood
In which the burthen of the mystery,
In which the heavy and the weary weight
Of all this unintelligible world,
Is lightened: – that serene and blessed mood,
In which the affections gently lead us on, –
Until, the breath of this corporeal frame
And even the motion of our human blood
Almost suspended, we are laid asleep
In body, and become a living soul:
While with an eye made quiet by the power
Of harmony, and the deep power of joy,
We see into the life of things.   ———— *mind*
                    If this
Be but a vain belief, yet, oh! how oft –
In darkness and amid the many shapes
Of joyless daylight; when the fretful stir
Unprofitable, and the fever of the world,
Have hung upon the beatings of my heart –
How oft, in spirit, have I turned to thee,
O sylvan Wye! thou wanderer thro' the woods,
How often has my spirit turned to thee!

    And now, with gleams of half-extinguished thought,
With many recognitions dim and faint,

And somewhat of a sad perplexity,
The picture of the mind revives again:
While here I stand, not only with the sense
Of present pleasure, but with pleasing thoughts
That in this moment there is life and food
For future years. And so I dare to hope,
Though changed, no doubt, from what I was when first
I came among these hills; when like a roe
I bounded o'er the mountains, by the sides
Of the deep rivers, and the lonely streams,
Wherever nature led: more like a man
Flying from something that he dreads than one
Who sought the thing he loved. For nature then
(The coarser pleasures of my boyish days,
And their glad animal movements all gone by)
To me was all in all. – I cannot paint
What then I was. The sounding cataract
Haunted me like a passion: the tall rock,
The mountain, and the deep and gloomy wood,
Their colours and their forms, were then to me
An appetite; a feeling and a love,
That had no need of a remoter charm,
By thought supplied, nor any interest
Unborrowed from the eye. – That time is past,
And all its aching joys are now no more,
And all its dizzy raptures. Not for this
Faint I, nor mourn nor murmur; other gifts
Have followed; for such loss, I would believe,
Abundant recompense. For I have learned
To look on nature, not as in the hour
Of thoughtless youth; but hearing oftentimes
The still, sad music of humanity,
Nor harsh nor grating, though of ample power
To chasten and subdue. And I have felt

A presence that disturbs me with the joy
Of elevated thoughts; a sense sublime
Of something far more deeply interfused,
Whose dwelling is the light of setting suns,
And the round ocean and the living air,
And the blue sky, and in the mind of man:
A motion and a spirit, that impels
All thinking things, all objects of all thought,
And rolls through all things. Therefore am I still
A lover of the meadows and the woods,
And mountains; and of all that we behold
From this green earth; of all the mighty world
Of eye, and ear, – both what they half create,
And what perceive; well pleased to recognise
In nature and the language of the sense
The anchor of my purest thoughts, the nurse,
The guide, the guardian of my heart, and soul
Of all my moral being.
                         Nor perchance,
If I were not thus taught, should I the more
Suffer my genial spirits to decay:
For thou art with me here upon the banks
Of this fair river; thou my dearest Friend,
My dear, dear Friend; and in thy voice I catch
The language of my former heart, and read
My former pleasures in the shooting lights
Of thy wild eyes. Oh! yet a little while
May I behold in thee what I was once,
My dear, dear Sister! and this prayer I make,
Knowing that Nature never did betray
The heart that loved her; 'tis her privilege,
Through all the years of this our life, to lead
From joy to joy: for she can so inform
The mind that is within us, so impress

With quietness and beauty, and so feed
With lofty thoughts, that neither evil tongues,
Rash judgments, nor the sneers of selfish men,
Nor greetings where no kindness is, nor all
The dreary intercourse of daily life,
Shall e'er prevail against us, or disturb
Our cheerful faith, that all which we behold
Is full of blessings. Therefore let the moon
Shine on thee in thy solitary walk;
And let the misty mountain-winds be free
To blow against thee: and, in after years,
When these wild ecstasies shall be matured
Into a sober pleasure; why thy mind
Shall be a mansion for all lovely forms,
Thy memory be as a dwelling-place
For all sweet sounds and harmonies; oh! then,
If solitude, or fear, or pain, or grief,
Should be thy portion, with what healing thoughts
Of tender joy wilt thou remember me,
And these my exhortations! Nor, perchance –
If I should be where I no more can hear
Thy voice, nor catch from thy wild eyes these gleams
Of past existence – wilt thou then forget
That on the banks of this delightful stream
We stood together; and that I, so long
A worshipper of Nature, hither came
Unwearied in that service: rather say
With warmer love – oh! with far deeper zeal
Of holier love. Nor wilt thou then forget,
That after many wanderings, many years
Of absence, these steep woods and lofty cliffs,
And this green pastoral landscape, were to me
More dear, both for themselves and for thy sake!

French Revolution

Oh! pleasant exercise of hope and joy!
For mighty were the auxiliars which then stood
Upon our side, we who were strong in love!
Bliss was it in that dawn to be alive,
But to be young was very heaven! – Oh! times,
In which the meagre, stale, forbidding ways
Of custom, law, and statute, took at once
The attraction of a country in romance!
When Reason seemed the most to assert her rights,
When most intent on making of herself
A prime Enchantress – to assist the work
Which then was going forward in her name!
Not favoured spots alone, but the whole earth,
The beauty wore of promise, that which sets
(As at some moment might not be unfelt
Among the bowers of paradise itself)
The budding rose above the rose full blown.
What temper at the prospect did not wake
To happiness unthought of? The inert
Were roused, and lively natures rapt away!
They who had fed their childhood upon dreams,
The playfellows of fancy, who had made
All powers of swiftness, subtilty, and strength
Their ministers, – who in lordly wise had stirred
Among the grandest objects of the sense,
And dealt with whatsoever they found there
As if they had within some lurking right
To wield it; – they, too, who, of gentle mood,
Had watched all gentle motions, and to these
Had fitted their own thoughts, schemers more mild,
And in the region of their peaceful selves; –

Now was it that both found, the meek and lofty
Did both find, helpers to their heart's desire,
And stuff at hand, plastic as they could wish;
Were called upon to exercise their skill,
Not in Utopia, subterranean fields,
Or some secreted island, Heaven knows where!
But in the very world, which is the world
Of all of us, – the place where in the end
We find our happiness, or not at all!

Dedication

Happy the feeling from the bosom thrown
In perfect shape (whose beauty Time shall spare
Though a breath made it) like a bubble blown
For summer pastime into wanton air;
Happy the thought best likened to a stone
Of the sea-beach, when, polished with nice care,
Veins it discovers exquisite and rare,
Which for the loss of that moist gleam atone
That tempted first to gather it. That here,
O chief of Friends! such feelings I present
To thy regard, with thoughts so fortunate,
Were a vain notion; but the hope is dear
That thou, if not with partial joy elate,
Wilt smile upon this gift with more than mild content!

Nuns fret not at their convent's narrow room

Nuns fret not at their convent's narrow room;
And hermits are contented with their cells;
And students with their pensive citadels;
Maids at the wheel, the weaver at his loom,
Sit blithe and happy; bees that soar for bloom,
High as the highest Peak of Furness-fells,
Will murmur by the hour in foxglove bells:
In truth the prison, unto which we doom
Ourselves, no prison is: and hence for me,
In sundry moods, 'twas pastime to be bound
Within the Sonnet's scanty plot of ground;
Pleased if some Souls (for such there needs must be)
Who have felt the weight of too much liberty,
Should find brief solace there, as I have found.

Why, Minstrel, these
untuneful murmurings

'Why, Minstrel, these untuneful murmurings –
Dull, flagging notes that with each other jar?'
'Think, gentle Lady, of a Harp so far
From its own country, and forgive the strings.'
A simple answer! but even so forth springs,
From the Castalian fountain of the heart,
The Poetry of Life, and all *that* Art
Divine of words quickening insensate things.
From the submissive necks of guiltless men
Stretched on the block the glittering axe recoils;
Sun, moon, and stars, all struggle in the toils
Of mortal sympathy; what wonder then
That the poor Harp distempered music yields
To its sad Lord, far from his native fields?

To Sleep

O gentle Sleep! do they belong to thee,
These twinklings of oblivion? Thou dost love
To sit in meekness, like the brooding Dove,
A captive never wishing to be free.
This tiresome night, O Sleep! thou art to me
A Fly, that up and down himself doth shove
Upon a fretful rivulet, now above,
Now on the water vexed with mockery.
I have no pain that calls for patience, no;
Hence am I cross and peevish as a child:
Am pleased by fits to have thee for my foe,
Yet ever willing to be reconciled:
O gentle Creature! do not use me so,
But once and deeply let me be beguiled.

To Sleep

A flock of sheep that leisurely pass by,
One after one; the sound of rain, and bees
Murmuring; the fall of rivers, winds and seas,
Smooth fields, white sheets of water, and pure sky;
I have thought of all by turns, and yet do lie
Sleepless! and soon the small birds' melodies
Must hear, first uttered from my orchard trees;
And the first cuckoo's melancholy cry.
Even thus last night, and two nights more, I lay,
And could not win thee, Sleep! by any stealth:
So do not let me wear to-night away:
Without Thee what is all the morning's wealth?
Come, blessed barrier between day and day,
Dear mother of fresh thoughts and joyous health!

Surprised by joy –
impatient as the Wind

Surprised by joy – impatient as the Wind
I turned to share the transport – Oh! with whom
But Thee, deep buried in the silent tomb,
That spot which no vicissitude can find?
Love, faithful love, recalled thee to my mind –
But how could I forget thee? Through what power,
Even for the least division of an hour,
Have I been so beguiled as to be blind
To my most grievous loss! – That thought's return
Was the worst pang that sorrow ever bore,
Save one, one only, when I stood forlorn,
Knowing my heart's best treasure was no more;
That neither present time, nor years unborn
Could to my sight that heavenly face restore.

It is a beauteous evening, calm and free

It is a beauteous evening, calm and free,
The holy time is quiet as a Nun
Breathless with adoration; the broad sun
Is sinking down in its tranquillity;
The gentleness of heaven broods o'er the Sea:
Listen! the mighty Being is awake,
And doth with his eternal motion make
A sound like thunder – everlastingly.
Dear Child! dear Girl! that walkest with me here,
If thou appear untouched by solemn thought,
Thy nature is not therefore less divine:
Thou liest in Abraham's bosom all the year;
And worshipp'st at the Temple's inner shrine,
God being with thee when we know it not.

The world is too much with us; late and soon

The world is too much with us; late and soon,
Getting and spending, we lay waste our powers:
Little we see in Nature that is ours;
We have given our hearts away, a sordid boon!
This Sea that bares her bosom to the moon;
The winds that will be howling at all hours,
And are up-gathered now like sleeping flowers;
For this, for everything, we are out of tune;
It moves us not. – Great God! I'd rather be
A Pagan suckled in a creed outworn;
So might I, standing on this pleasant lea,
Have glimpses that would make me less forlorn;
Have sight of Proteus rising from the sea;
Or hear old Triton blow his wreathèd horn.

Retirement

If the whole weight of what we think and feel,
Save only far as thought and feeling blend
With action, were as nothing, patriot Friend!
From thy remonstrance would be no appeal;
But to promote and fortify the weal
Of her own Being is her paramount end;
A truth which they alone shall comprehend
Who shun the mischief which they cannot heal.
Peace in these feverish times is sovereign bliss:
Here, with no thirst but what the stream can slake,
And startled only by the rustling brake,
Cool air I breathe; while the unincumbered Mind,
By some weak aims at services assigned
To gentle Natures, thanks not Heaven amiss.

Those words were uttered
as in pensive mood

    – 'they are of the sky,
    And from our earthly memory fade away.'

Those words were uttered as in pensive mood
We turned, departing from that solemn sight:
A contrast and reproach to gross delight,
And life's unspiritual pleasures daily wooed!
But now upon this thought I cannot brood;
It is unstable as a dream of night;
Nor will I praise a cloud, however bright,
Disparaging Man's gifts, and proper food.
Grove, isle, with every shape of sky-built dome,
Though clad in colours beautiful and pure,
Find in the heart of man no natural home:
The immortal Mind craves objects that endure:
These cleave to it; from these it cannot roam,
Nor they from it: their fellowship is secure.

September, 1815

While not a leaf seems faded; while the fields,
With ripening harvest prodigally fair,
In the brightest sunshine bask; this nipping air,
Sent from some distant clime where Winter wields
His icy scimitar, a foretaste yields
Of bitter change, and bids the flowers beware;
And whispers to the silent birds, 'Prepare
Against the threatening foe your trustiest shields.'
For me, who under kindlier laws belong
To Nature's tuneful quire, this rustling dry
Through leaves yet green, and yon crystalline sky,
Announce a season potent to renew,
'Mid frost and snow, the instinctive joys of song,
And nobler cares than listless summer knew.

November 1

How clear, how keen, how marvellously bright
The effluence from yon distant mountain's head,
Which, strewn with snow smooth as the sky can shed,
Shines like another sun – on mortal sight
Uprisen, as if to check approaching Night,
And all her twinkling stars. Who now would tread,
If so he might, yon mountain's glittering head –
Terrestrial, but a surface, by the flight
Of sad mortality's earth-sullying wing,
Unswept, unstained? Nor shall the aerial Powers
Dissolve that beauty, destined to endure,
White, radiant, spotless, exquisitely pure,
Through all vicissitudes, till genial Spring
Has filled the laughing vales with welcome flowers.

Composed During a Storm

One who was suffering tumult in his soul
Yet failed to seek the sure relief of prayer,
Went forth – his course surrendering to the care
Of the fierce wind, while mid-day lightnings prowl
Insidiously, untimely thunders growl;
While trees, dim-seen, in frenzied numbers, tear
The lingering remnant of their yellow hair,
And shivering wolves, surprised with darkness, howl
As if the sun were not. He raised his eye
Soul-smitten; for, that instant did appear
Large space ('mid dreadful clouds) of purest sky,
An azure disc – shield of Tranquillity;
Invisible, unlooked-for, minister
Of providential goodness ever nigh!

Though narrow be that old Man's cares, and near

> – 'gives to airy nothing
> A local habitation and a name.'

Though narrow be that old Man's cares, and near,
The poor old Man is greater than he seems:
For he hath waking empire, wide as dreams;
An ample sovereignty of eye and ear.
Rich are his walks with supernatural cheer;
The region of his inner spirit teems
With vital sounds and monitory gleams
Of high astonishment and pleasing fear.
He the seven birds hath seen, that never part,
Seen the SEVEN WHISTLERS in their nightly rounds,
And counted them: and oftentimes will start –
For overhead are sweeping GABRIEL'S HOUNDS,
Doomed, with their impious Lord, the flying Hart
To chase for ever, on aërial grounds!

Four fiery steeds impatient of the rein

Four fiery steeds impatient of the rein
Whirled us o'er sunless ground beneath a sky
As void of sunshine, when, from that wide plain,
Clear tops of far-off mountains we descry,
Like a Sierra of cerulean Spain,
All light and lustre. Did no heart reply?
Yes, there was One; – for One, asunder fly
The thousand links of that ethereal chain;
And green vales open out, with grove and field,
And the fair front of many a happy Home;
Such tempting spots as into vision come
While Soldiers, weary of the arms they wield
And sick at heart of strifeful Christendom,
Gaze on the moon by parting clouds revealed.

Composed upon Westminster Bridge, September 3, 1802

Earth has not anything to show more fair:
Dull would he be of soul who could pass by
A sight so touching in its majesty:
This City now doth, like a garment, wear
The beauty of the morning; silent, bare,
Ships, towers, domes, theatres, and temples lie
Open unto the fields, and to the sky;
All bright and glittering in the smokeless air.
Never did sun more beautifully steep
In his first splendour, valley, rock, or hill;
Ne'er saw I, never felt, a calm so deep!
The river glideth at his own sweet will:
Dear God! the very houses seem asleep;
And all that mighty heart is lying still!

When Philoctetes in the Lemnian isle

When Philoctetes in the Lemnian isle
Like a Form sculptured on a monument
Lay couched; on him or his dread bow unbent
Some wild Bird oft might settle and beguile
The rigid features of a transient smile,
Disperse the tear, or to the sigh give vent,
Slackening the pains of ruthless banishment
From his lov'd home, and from heroic toil.
And trust that spiritual Creatures round us move,
Griefs to allay which Reason cannot heal;
Yea, veriest reptiles have sufficed to prove
To fettered wretchedness, that no Bastille
Is deep enough to exclude the light of love,
Though man for brother man has ceased to feel.

While Anna's peers and early playmates tread

While Anna's peers and early playmates tread,
In freedom, mountain-turf and river's marge;
Or float with music in the festal barge;
Rein the proud steed, or through the dance are led;
Her doom it is to press a weary bed –
Till oft her guardian Angel, to some charge
More urgent called, will stretch his wings at large,
And friends too rarely prop the languid head.
Yet, helped by Genius – untired comforter,
The presence even of a stuffed Owl for her
Can cheat the time; sending her fancy out
To ivied castles and to moonlight skies,
Though he can neither stir a plume, nor shout;
Nor veil, with restless film, his staring eyes.

To —

'Miss not the occasion: by the forelock take
That subtle Power, the never-halting Time,
Lest a mere moment's putting-off should make
Mischance almost as heavy as a crime.'

'Wait, prithee, wait!' this answer Lesbia threw
Forth to her Dove, and took no further heed.
Her eye was busy, while her fingers flew
Across the harp, with soul-engrossing speed;
But from that bondage when her thoughts were freed
She rose, and toward the close-shut casement drew,
Whence the poor unregarded Favourite, true
To old affections, had been heard to plead
With flapping wing for entrance. What a shriek
Forced from that voice so lately tuned to a strain
Of harmony! – a shriek of terror, pain,
And self-reproach! for, from aloft, a Kite
Pounced, – and the Dove, which from its ruthless beak
She could not rescue, perished in her sight!

The Infant M— M—

Unquiet Childhood here by special grace
Forgets her nature, opening like a flower
That neither feeds nor wastes its vital power
In painful struggles. Months each other chase,
And nought untunes that Infant's voice; no trace
Of fretful temper sullies her pure cheek;
Prompt, lively, self-sufficing, yet so meek
That one enrapt with gazing on her face
(Which even the placid innocence of death
Could scarcely make more placid, heaven more bright)
Might learn to picture, for the eye of faith,
The Virgin, as she shone with kindred light;
A nursling couched upon her mother's knee,
Beneath some shady palm of Galilee.

A Poet! – He hath put his heart to school

A Poet! – He hath put his heart to school,
Nor dares to move unpropped upon the staff
Which Art hath lodged within his hand – must laugh
By precept only, and shed tears by rule.
Thy Art be Nature; the live current quaff,
And let the groveller sip his stagnant pool,
In fear that else, when Critics grave and cool
Have killed him, Scorn should write his epitaph.
How does the Meadow-flower its bloom unfold?
Because the lovely little flower is free
Down to its root, and, in that freedom, bold;
And so the grandeur of the Forest-tree
Comes not by casting in a formal mould,
But from its *own* divine vitality.

The most alluring clouds
that mount the sky

The most alluring clouds that mount the sky
Owe to a troubled element their forms,
Their hues to sunset. If with raptured eye
We watch their splendor, shall we covet storms,
And wish the Lord of day his slow decline
Would hasten, that such pomp may float on high?
Behold, already they forget to shine,
Dissolve – and leave to him who gazed a sigh.
Not loth to thank each moment for its boon
Of pure delight, come whensoe'er it may,
Peace let us seek, – to stedfast things attune
Calm expectations, leaving to the gay
And volatile their love of transient bowers,
The house that cannot pass away be ours.

Oh what a Wreck! how changed
in mien and speech!

Oh what a Wreck! how changed in mien and speech!
Yet – though dread Powers, that work in mystery, spin
Entanglings of the brain; though shadows stretch
O'er the chilled heart – reflect; far, far within
Hers is a holy Being, freed from Sin.
She is not what she seems, a forlorn wretch,
But delegated Spirits comforts fetch
To Her from heights that Reason may not win.
Like Children, She is privileged to hold
Divine communion; both to live and move,
Whate'er to shallow Faith their ways unfold,
Inly illumined by Heaven's pitying love;
Love pitying innocence, not long to last,
In them – in Her our sins and sorrows past.

In my mind's eye a Temple,
like a cloud

In my mind's eye a Temple, like a cloud
Slowly surmounting some invidious hill,
Rose out of darkness: the bright Work stood still;
And might of its own beauty have been proud,
But it was fashioned and to God was vowed
By Virtues that diffused, in every part,
Spirit divine through forms of human art:
Faith had her arch – her arch, when winds blow loud,
Into the consciousness of safety thrilled;
And Love her towers of dread foundation laid
Under the grave of things; Hope had her spire
Star-high, and pointing still to something higher;
Trembling I gazed, but heard a voice – it said,
'Hell-gates are powerless Phantoms when *we* build.'

At Furness Abbey

Well have yon Railway Labourers to THIS ground
Withdrawn for noontide rest. They sit, they walk
Among the Ruins, but no idle talk
Is heard; to grave demeanour all are bound;
And from one voice a Hymn with tuneful sound
Hallows once more the long-deserted Quire
And thrills the old sepulchral earth, around.
Others look up, and with fixed eyes admire
That wide-spanned arch, wondering how it was raised,
To keep, so high in air, its strength and grace:
All seem to feel the spirit of the place,
And by the general reverence God is praised:
Profane Despoilers, stand ye not reproved,
While thus these simple-hearted men are moved?

At the Grave of Burns, 1803

SEVEN YEARS AFTER HIS DEATH

I shiver, Spirit fierce and bold,
At thought of what I now behold:
As vapours breathed from dungeons cold
  Strike pleasure dead,
So sadness comes from out the mould
  Where Burns is laid.

And have I then thy bones so near,
And thou forbidden to appear?
As if it were thyself that's here
  I shrink with pain;
And both my wishes and my fear
  Alike are vain.

Off weight – nor press on weight! – away
Dark thoughts! – they came, but not to stay;
With chastened feelings would I pay
  The tribute due
To him, and aught that hides his clay
  From mortal view.

Fresh as the flower, whose modest worth
He sang, his genius 'glinted' forth,
Rose like a star that touching earth,
  For so it seems,
Doth glorify its humble birth
  With matchless beams.

The piercing eye, the thoughtful brow,
The struggling heart, where be they now? –
Full soon the Aspirant of the plough,
    The prompt, the brave,
Slept, with the obscurest, in the low
    And silent grave.

I mourned with thousands, but as one
More deeply grieved, for He was gone
Whose light I hailed when first it shone,
    And showed my youth
How Verse may build a princely throne
    On humble truth.

Alas! where'er the current tends,
Regret pursues and with it blends, –
Huge Criffel's hoary top ascends
    By Skiddaw seen, –
Neighbours we were, and loving friends
    We might have been;

True friends though diversely inclined;
But heart with heart and mind with mind,
Where the main fibres are entwined,
    Through Nature's skill,
May even by contraries be joined
    More closely still.

The tear will start, and let it flow;
Thou 'poor Inhabitant below,'
At this dread moment – even so –
    Might we together
Have sate and talked where gowans blow,
    Or on wild heather.

What treasures would have then been placed
Within my reach; of knowledge graced
By fancy what a rich repast!
     But why go on? –
Oh! spare to sweep, thou mournful blast,
     His grave grass-grown.

There, too, a Son, his joy and pride,
(Not three weeks past the Stripling died,)
Lies gathered to his Father's side,
     Soul-moving sight!
Yet one to which is not denied
     Some sad delight.

For *he* is safe, a quiet bed
Hath early found among the dead,
Harboured where none can be misled,
     Wronged, or distrest;
And surely here it may be said
     That such are blest.

And oh for Thee, by pitying grace
Checked oft-times in a devious race,
May He, who halloweth the place
     Where Man is laid,
Receive thy Spirit in the embrace
     For which it prayed!

Sighing I turned away; but ere
Night fell I heard, or seemed to hear,
Music that sorrow comes not near,
     A ritual hymn,
Chanted in love that casts out fear
     By Seraphim.

The Solitary Reaper

Behold her, single in the field,
Yon solitary Highland Lass!
Reaping and singing by herself;
Stop here, or gently pass!
Alone she cuts and binds the grain,
And sings a melancholy strain;
O listen! for the Vale profound
Is overflowing with the sound.

No Nightingale did ever chaunt
More welcome notes to weary bands
Of travellers in some shady haunt,
Among Arabian sands:
A voice so thrilling ne'er was heard
In spring-time from the Cuckoo-bird,
Breaking the silence of the seas
Among the farthest Hebrides.

Will no one tell me what she sings? –
Perhaps the plaintive numbers flow
For old, unhappy, far-off things,
And battles long ago:
Or is it some more humble lay,
Familiar matter of to-day?
Some natural sorrow, loss, or pain,
That has been, and may be again?

Whate'er the theme, the Maiden sang
As if her song could have no ending;
I saw her singing at her work,
And o'er the sickle bending: –

I listened, motionless and still;
And, as I mounted up the hill,
The music in my heart I bore,
Long after it was heard no more.

Composed in the Valley near Dover, on the Day of Landing

Here, on our native soil, we breathe once more.
The cock that crows, the smoke that curls, that sound
Of bells; – those boys who in yon meadow-ground
In white-sleeved shirts are playing; and the roar
Of the waves breaking on the chalky shore; –
All, all are English. Oft have I looked round
With joy in Kent's green vales; but never found
Myself so satisfied in heart before.
Europe is yet in bonds; but let that pass,
Thought for another moment. Thou art free,
My Country! and 'tis joy enough and pride
For one hour's perfect bliss, to tread the grass
Of England once again, and hear and see,
With such a dear Companion at my side.

London, 1802

Milton! thou shouldst be living at this hour:
England hath need of thee: she is a fen
Of stagnant waters: altar, sword, and pen,
Fireside, the heroic wealth of hall and bower,
Have forfeited their ancient English dower
Of inward happiness. We are selfish men;
Oh! raise us up, return to us again;
And give us manners, virtue, freedom, power.
Thy soul was like a Star, and dwelt apart;
Thou hadst a voice whose sound was like the sea:
Pure as the naked heavens, majestic, free,
So didst thou travel on life's common way,
In cheerful godliness; and yet thy heart
The lowliest duties on herself did lay.

Avaunt all specious pliancy of mind

Avaunt all specious pliancy of mind
In men of low degree, all smooth pretence!
I better like a blunt indifference,
And self-respecting slowness, disinclined
To win me at first sight: and be there joined
Patience and temperance with this high reserve,
Honour that knows the path and will not swerve;
Affections which, if put to proof, are kind;
And piety towards God. Such men of old
Were England's native growth; and, throughout Spain,
(Thanks to high God) forests of such remain:
Then for that Country let our hopes be bold;
For matched with these shall policy prove vain,
Her arts, her strength, her iron, and her gold.

The French and the
Spanish Guerillas

Hunger, and sultry heat, and nipping blast
From bleak hill-top, and length of march by night
Through heavy swamp, or over snow-clad height –
These hardships ill-sustained, these dangers past,
The roving Spanish Bands are reached at last,
Charged, and dispersed like foam: but as a flight
Of scattered quails by signs do reunite,
So these, – and, heard of once again, are chased
With combinations of long-practised art
And newly-kindled hope; but they are fled –
Gone are they, viewless as the buried dead:
Where now? – Their sword is at the Foeman's heart!
And thus from year to year his walk they thwart,
And hang like dreams around his guilty bed.

Composed in One of the Catholic Cantons

Doomed as we are our native dust
To wet with many a bitter shower,
It ill befits us to disdain
The altar, to deride the fane,
Where simple Sufferers bend, in trust
To win a happier hour.

I love, where spreads the village lawn,
Upon some knee-worn cell to gaze:
Hail to the firm unmoving cross,
Aloft, where pines their branches toss!
And to the chapel far withdrawn,
That lurks by lonely ways!

Where'er we roam – along the brink
Of Rhine – or by the sweeping Po,
Through Alpine vale, or champaign wide,
Whate'er we look on, at our side
Be Charity! – to bid us think,
And feel, if we would know.

Sky-Prospect –
from the Plain of France

Lo! in the burning west, the craggy nape
Of a proud Ararat! and, thereupon,
The Ark, her melancholy voyage done!
Yon rampant cloud mimics a lion's shape;
There, combats a huge crocodile – agape
A golden spear to swallow! and that brown
And massy grove, so near yon blazing town,
Stirs and recedes – destruction to escape!
Yet all is harmless – as the Elysian shades
Where Spirits dwell in undisturbed repose –
Silently disappears, or quickly fades:
Meek Nature's evening comment on the shows
That for oblivion take their daily birth
From all the fuming vanities of Earth!

On Being Stranded
near the Harbour of Boulogne

Why cast ye back upon the Gallic shore,
Ye furious waves! a patriotic Son
Of England – who in hope her coast had won,
His project crowned, his pleasant travel o'er?
Well – let him pace this noted beach once more,
That gave the Roman his triumphal shells;
That saw the Corsican his cap and bells
Haughtily shake, a dreaming Conqueror! –
Enough: my Country's cliffs I can behold,
And proudly think, beside the chafing sea,
Of checked ambition, tyranny controlled,
And folly cursed with endless memory:
These local recollections ne'er can cloy;
Such ground I from my very heart enjoy!

At Rome

Is this, ye Gods, the Capitolian Hill?
Yon petty Steep in truth the fearful Rock,
Tarpeian named of yore, and keeping still
That name, a local Phantom proud to mock
The Traveller's expectation? – Could our Will
Destroy the ideal Power within, 'twere done
Thro' what men see and touch, – slaves wandering on,
Impelled by thirst of all but Heaven-taught skill.
Full oft, our wish obtained, deeply we sigh;
Yet not unrecompensed are they who learn,
From that depression raised, to mount on high
With stronger wing, more clearly to discern
Eternal things; and, if need be, defy
Change, with a brow not insolent, though stern.

Near the Same Lake

For action born, existing to be tried,
Powers manifold we have that intervene
To stir the heart that would too closely screen
Her peace from images to pain allied.
What wonder if at midnight, by the side
Of Sanguinetto or broad Thrasymene,
The clang of arms is heard, and phantoms glide,
Unhappy ghosts in troops by moonlight seen;
And singly thine, O vanquished Chief! whose corse,
Unburied, lay hid under heaps of slain:
But who is He? – the Conqueror. Would he force
His way to Rome? Ah, no, – round hill and plain
Wandering, he haunts, at fancy's strong command,
This spot – his shadowy death-cup in his hand.

The Cuckoo at Laverna

May 25, 1837

List – 'twas the Cuckoo. – O with what delight
Heard I that voice! and catch it now, though faint,
Far off and faint, and melting into air,
Yet not to be mistaken. Hark again!
Those louder cries give notice that the Bird,
Although invisible as Echo's self,
Is wheeling hitherward. Thanks, happy Creature,
For this unthought-of greeting!
                                    While allured
From vale to hill, from hill to vale led on,
We have pursued, through various lands, a long
And pleasant course; flower after flower has blown,
Embellishing the ground that gave them birth
With aspects novel to my sight; but still
Most fair, most welcome, when they drank the dew
In a sweet fellowship with kinds beloved,
For old remembrance sake. And oft – where Spring
Display'd her richest blossoms among files
Of orange-trees bedecked with glowing fruit
Ripe for the hand, or under a thick shade
Of Ilex, or, if better suited to the hour,
The lightsome Olive's twinkling canopy –
Oft have I heard the Nightingale and Thrush
Blending as in a common English grove
Their love-songs; but, where'er my feet might roam,
Whate'er assemblages of new and old,
Strange and familiar, might beguile the way,
A gratulation from that vagrant Voice
Was wanting; – and most happily till now.

For see, Laverna! mark the far-famed Pile,
High on the brink of that precipitous rock,
Implanted like a Fortress, as in truth
It is, a Christian Fortress, garrisoned
In faith and hope, a dutiful obedience,
By a few Monks, a stern society,
Dead to the world and scorning earth-born joys.
Nay – though the hopes that drew, the fears that drove,
St Francis, far from Man's resort, to abide
Among these sterile heights of Apennine,
Bound him, nor, since he raised yon House, have ceased
To bind his spiritual Progeny, with rules
Stringent as flesh can tolerate and live;
His milder Genius (thanks to the good God
That made us) over those severe restraints
Of mind, that dread heart-freezing discipline,
Doth sometimes here predominate, and works
By unsought means for gracious purposes;
For earth through heaven, for heaven, by changeful earth,
Illustrated, and mutually endeared.

Rapt though He were above the power of sense,
Familiarly, yet out of the cleansed heart
Of that once sinful Being overflowed
On sun, moon, stars, the nether elements,
And every shape of creature they sustain,
Divine affections; and with beast and bird
(Stilled from afar – such marvel story tells –
By casual outbreak of his passionate words,
And from their own pursuits in field or grove
Drawn to his side by look or act of love
Humane, and virtue of his innocent life)
He wont to hold companionship so free,
So pure, so fraught with knowledge and delight,

As to be likened in his Followers' minds
To that which our first Parents, ere the fall
From their high state darkened the Earth with fear,
Held with all Kinds in Eden's blissful bowers.

  Then question not that, 'mid the austere Band,
Who breathe the air he breathed, tread where he trod,
Some true Partakers of his loving spirit
Do still survive, and, with those gentle hearts
Consorted, Others, in the power, the faith,
Of a baptized imagination, prompt
To catch from Nature's humblest monitors
Whate'er they bring of impulses sublime.

  Thus sensitive must be the Monk, though pale
With fasts, with vigils worn, depressed by years,
Whom in a sunny glade I chanced to see,
Upon a pine-tree's storm-uprooted trunk,
Seated alone, with forehead sky-ward raised,
Hands clasped above the crucifix he wore
Appended to his bosom, and lips closed
By the joint pressure of his musing mood
And habit of his vow. That ancient Man –
Nor haply less the Brother whom I marked,
As we approached the Convent gate, aloft
Looking far forth from his aerial cell,
A young Ascetic – Poet, Hero, Sage,
He might have been, Lover belike he was –
If they received into a conscious ear
The notes whose first faint greeting startled me,
Whose sedulous iteration thrilled with joy
My heart – may have been moved like me to think,
Ah! not like me who walk in the world's ways,
On the great Prophet, styled *the Voice of One*

Crying amid the wilderness, and given,
Now that their snows must melt, their herbs and flowers
Revive, their obstinate winter pass away,
That awful name to Thee, thee, simple Cuckoo,
Wandering in solitude, and evermore
Foretelling and proclaiming, ere thou leave
This thy last haunt beneath Italian skies
To carry thy glad tidings over heights
Still loftier, and to climes more near the Pole.

Voice of the Desert, fare-thee-well; sweet Bird!
If that substantial title please thee more,
Farewell! – but go thy way, no need hast thou
Of a good wish sent after thee; from bower
To bower as green, from sky to sky as clear,
Thee gentle breezes waft – or airs that meet
Thy course and sport around thee softly fan –
Till Night, descending upon hill and vale,
Grants to thy mission a brief term of silence,
And folds thy pinions up in blest repose.

At the Convent of Camaldoli

Grieve for the Man who hither came bereft,
And seeking consolation from above;
Nor grieve the less that skill to him was left
To paint this picture of his lady-love:
Can she, a blessèd saint, the work approve?
And O, good Brethren of the cowl, a thing
So fair, to which with peril he must cling,
Destroy in pity, or with care remove.
That bloom – those eyes – can they assist to bind
Thoughts that would stray from Heaven? The dream must
   cease
To be; by Faith, not sight, his soul must live;
Else will the enamoured Monk too surely find
How wide a space can part from inward peace
The most profound repose his cell can give.

Continued

The world forsaken, all its busy cares
And stirring interests shunned with desperate flight,
All trust abandoned in the healing might
Of virtuous action; all that courage dares,
Labour accomplishes, or patience bears –
Those helps rejected, they, whose minds perceive
How subtly works man's weakness, sighs may heave
For such a One beset with cloistral snares.
Father of Mercy! rectify his view,
If with his vows this object ill agree;
Shed over it Thy grace, and thus subdue
Imperious passion in a heart set free: –
That earthly love may to herself be true,
Give him a soul that cleaveth unto Thee.

Among the Ruins
of a Convent in the Apennines

Ye Trees! whose slender roots entwine
   Altars that piety neglects;
Whose infant arms enclasp the shrine
   Which no devotion now respects;
If not a straggler from the herd
Here ruminate, nor shrouded bird,
Chanting her low-voiced hymn, take pride
In aught that ye would grace or hide –
How sadly is your love misplaced,
Fair Trees, your bounty run to waste!

Ye, too, wild Flowers, that no one heeds,
And ye – full often spurned as weeds –
In beauty clothed, or breathing sweetness
From fractured arch and mouldering wall –
Do but more touchingly recal
Man's headstrong violence and Time's fleetness,
Making the precincts ye adorn
Appear to sight still more forlorn.

Return, Content!
for fondly I pursued

Return, Content! for fondly I pursued,
Even when a child, the Streams – unheard, unseen;
Through tangled woods, impending rocks between;
Or, free as air, with flying inquest viewed
The sullen reservoirs whence their bold brood –
Pure as the morning, fretful, boisterous, keen,
Green as the salt-sea billows, white and green –
Poured down the hills, a choral multitude!
Nor have I tracked their course for scanty gains;
They taught me random cares and truant joys,
That shield from mischief and preserve from stains
Vague minds, while men are growing out of boys;
Maturer Fancy owes to their rough noise
Impetuous thoughts that brook not servile reins.

from The River Duddon

AFTER-THOUGHT

…I thought of Thee, my partner and my guide,
As being past away. – Vain sympathies!
For, backward, Duddon! as I cast my eyes,
I see what was, and is, and will abide;
Still glides the Stream, and shall for ever glide;
The Form remains, the Function never dies;
While we, the brave, the mighty, and the wise,
We Men, who in our morn of youth defied
The elements, must vanish; – be it so!
Enough, if something from our hands have power
To live, and act, and serve the future hour;
And if, as toward the silent tomb we go,
Through love, through hope, and faith's transcendent
    dower,
We feel that we are greater than we know.

The pibroch's note, discountenanced or mute

The pibroch's note, discountenanced or mute;
The Roman kilt, degraded to a toy
Of quaint apparel for a half-spoilt boy;
The target mouldering like ungathered fruit;
The smoking steam-boat eager in pursuit,
As eagerly pursued; the umbrella spread
To weather-fend the Celtic herdsman's head –
All speak of manners withering to the root,
And of old honours, too, and passions high:
Then may we ask, though pleased that thought should range
Among the conquests of civility,
Survives imagination – to the change
Superior? Help to virtue does she give?
If not, O Mortals, better cease to live!

Composed in the Glen of Loch Etive

'This Land of Rainbows spanning glens whose walls,
Rock-built, are hung with rainbow-coloured mists –
Of far-stretched Meres whose salt flood never rests –
Of tuneful Caves and playful Waterfalls –
Of Mountains varying momently their crests –
Proud be this Land! whose poorest huts are halls
Where Fancy entertains becoming guests;
While native song the heroic Past recals.'
Thus, in the net of her own wishes caught,
The Muse exclaimed; but Story now must hide
Her trophies, Fancy crouch; the course of pride
Has been diverted, other lessons taught,
That make the Patriot-spirit bow her head
Where the all-conquering Roman feared to tread.

Eagles

Dishonoured Rock and Ruin! that, by law
Tyrannic, keep the Bird of Jove embarred
Like a lone criminal whose life is spared.
Vexed is he, and screams loud. The last I saw
Was on the wing; stooping, he struck with awe
Man, bird, and beast; then, with a consort paired,
From a bold headland, their loved aery's guard,
Flew high above Atlantic waves, to draw
Light from the fountain of the setting sun.
Such was this Prisoner once; and when his plumes
The sea-blast ruffles as the storm comes on,
Then, for a moment, he, in spirit, resumes
His rank 'mong freeborn creatures that live free,
His power, his beauty, and his majesty.

Suggested at Tyndrum in a Storm

Enough of garlands, of the Arcadian crook,
And all that Greece and Italy have sung
Of Swains reposing myrtle groves among!
Ours couch on naked rocks, – will cross a brook
Swoln with chill rains, nor ever cast a look
This way or that, or give it even a thought
More than by smoothest pathway may be brought
Into a vacant mind. Can written book
Teach what *they* learn? Up, hardy Mountaineer!
And guide the Bard, ambitious to be One
Of Nature's privy council, as thou art,
On cloud-sequestered heights, that see and hear
To what dread Powers He delegates his part
On Earth, who works in the heaven of heavens, alone.

'Rest and Be Thankful'

At the Head of Glencroe

Doubling and doubling with laborious walk,
Who, that has gained at length the wished-for Height,
This brief this simple wayside Call can slight,
And rests not thankful? Whether cheered by talk
With some loved friend, or by the unseen hawk
Whistling to clouds and sky-born streams, that shine
At the sun's outbreak, as with light divine,
Ere they descend to nourish root and stalk
Of valley flowers. Nor, while the limbs repose,
Will we forget that, as the fowl can keep
Absolute stillness, poised aloft in air,
And fishes front, unmoved, the torrent's sweep, –
So may the Soul, through powers that Faith bestows,
Win rest, and ease, and peace, with bliss that Angels share.

The Highland Broach

The exact resemblance which the old Broach (still in use, though rarely met with, among the Highlanders) bears to the Roman Fibula must strike everyone, and concurs with the plaid and kilt to recall to mind the communication which the ancient Romans had with this remote country.

If to Tradition faith be due,
And echoes from old verse speak true,
Ere the meek Saint, Columba, bore
Glad tidings to Iona's shore,
No common light of nature blessed
The mountain region of the west,
A land where gentle manners ruled
O'er men in dauntless virtues schooled,
That raised, for centuries, a bar
Impervious to the tide of war:
Yet peaceful Arts did entrance gain
Where haughty Force had striven in vain;
And, 'mid the works of skilful hands,
By wanderers brought from foreign lands
And various climes, was not unknown
The clasp that fixed the Roman Gown;
The Fibula, whose shape, I ween,
Still in the Highland Broach is seen,
The silver Broach of massy frame,
Worn at the breast of some grave Dame
On road or path, or at the door
Of fern-thatched hut on heathy moor:
But delicate of yore its mould,
And the material finest gold;
As might beseem the fairest Fair,

Whether she graced a royal chair,
Or shed, within a vaulted hall,
No fancied lustre on the wall
Where shields of mighty heroes hung,
While Fingal heard what Ossian sung.

The heroic Age expired – it slept
Deep in its tomb: – the bramble crept
O'er Fingal's hearth; the grassy sod
Grew on the floors his sons had trod:
Malvina! where art thou? Their state
The noblest-born must abdicate;
The fairest, while with fire and sword
Come Spoilers – horde impelling horde,
Must walk the sorrowing mountains, drest
By ruder hands in homelier vest.
Yet still the female bosom lent,
And loved to borrow, ornament;
Still was its inner world a place
Reached by the dews of heavenly grace;
Still pity to this last retreat
Clove fondly; to his favourite seat
Love wound his way by soft approach,
Beneath a massier Highland Broach.

When alternations came of rage
Yet fiercer, in a darker age;
And feuds, where, clan encountering clan,
The weaker perished to a man;
For maid and mother, when despair
Might else have triumphed, baffling prayer,
One small possession lacked not power,
Provided in a calmer hour,
To meet such need as might befal –

Roof, raiment, bread, or burial:
For woman, even of tears bereft,
The hidden silver Broach was left.

As generations come and go,
Their arts, their customs, ebb and flow;
Fate, fortune, sweep strong powers away,
And feeble, of themselves, decay;
What poor abodes the heir-loom hide,
In which the castle once took pride!
Tokens, once kept as boasted wealth,
If saved at all, are saved by stealth.
Lo! ships, from seas by nature barred,
Mount along ways by man prepared;
And in far-stretching vales, whose streams
Seek other seas, their canvass gleams.
Lo! busy towns spring up, on coasts
Thronged yesterday by airy ghosts;
Soon, like a lingering star forlorn
Among the novelties of morn,
While young delights on old encroach,
Will vanish the last Highland Broach.

But when, from out their viewless bed,
Like vapours, years have rolled and spread;
And this poor verse, and worthier lays,
Shall yield no light of love or praise;
Then, by the spade, or cleaving plough,
Or torrent from the mountain's brow,
Or whirlwind, reckless what his might
Entombs, or forces into light;
Blind Chance, a volunteer ally,
That oft befriends Antiquity,
And clears Oblivion from reproach,
May render back the Highland Broach.

Roman Antiquities

(From the Roman Station at Old Penrith)

How profitless the relics that we cull,
Troubling the last holds of ambitious Rome,
Unless they chasten fancies that presume
Too high, or idle agitations lull!
Of the world's flatteries if the brain be full,
To have no seat for thought were better doom,
Like this old helmet, or the eyeless skull
Of him who gloried in its nodding plume.
Heaven out of view, our wishes what are they?
Our fond regrets tenacious in their grasp?
The Sage's theory? the Poet's lay? —
Mere Fibulæ without a robe to clasp;
Obsolete lamps, whose light no time recals;
Urns without ashes, tearless lacrymals!

from The White Doe of Rylstone

   'Action is transitory – a step, a blow,
The motion of a muscle – this way or that –
'Tis done; and in the after-vacancy
We wonder at ourselves like men betrayed:
Suffering is permanent, obscure and dark,
And has the nature of infinity.
Yet through that darkness (infinite though it seem
And irremoveable) gracious openings lie,
By which the soul – with patient steps of thought
Now toiling, wafted now on wings of prayer –
May pass in hope, and, though from mortal bonds
Yet undelivered, rise with sure ascent
Even to the fountain-head of peace divine.'

Crusades

The turbaned Race are poured in thickening swarms
Along the west; though driven from Aquitaine,
The Crescent glitters on the towers of Spain;
And soft Italia feels renewed alarms;
The scimitar, that yields not to the charms
Of ease, the narrow Bosphorus will disdain;
Nor long (that crossed) would Grecian hills detain
Their tents, and check the current of their arms.
Then blame not those who, by the mightiest lever
Known to the moral world, Imagination,
Upheave, so seems it, from her natural station
All Christendom: – they sweep along (was never
So huge a host!) – to tear from the Unbeliever
The precious Tomb, their haven of salvation.

Places of Worship

As star that shines dependent upon star
Is to the sky while we look up in love;
As to the deep fair ships which though they move
Seem fixed, to eyes that watch them from afar;
As to the sandy desert fountains are,
With palm-groves shaded at wide intervals,
Whose fruit around the sun-burnt Native falls
Of roving tired or desultory war –
Such to this British Isle her christian Fanes,
Each linked to each for kindred services;
Her Spires, her Steeple-towers with glittering vanes
Far-kenned, her Chapels lurking among trees,
Where a few villagers on bended knees
Find solace which a busy world disdains.

Mutability

From low to high doth dissolution climb,
And sink from high to low, along a scale
Of awful notes, whose concord shall not fail;
A musical but melancholy chime,
Which they can hear who meddle not with crime,
Nor avarice, nor over-anxious care.
Truth fails not; but her outward forms that bear
The longest date do melt like frosty rime,
That in the morning whitened hill and plain
And is no more; drop like the tower sublime
Of yesterday, which royally did wear
His crown of weeds, but could not even sustain
Some casual shout that broke the silent air,
Or the unimaginable touch of Time.

Soft as a cloud is yon blue Ridge – the Mere

Soft as a cloud is yon blue Ridge – the Mere
Seems firm as solid crystal, breathless, clear,
And motionless; and, to the gazer's eye,
Deeper than ocean, in the immensity
Of its vague mountains and unreal sky!
But, from the process in that still retreat,
Turn to minuter changes at our feet;
Observe how dewy Twilight has withdrawn
The crowd of daisies from the shaven lawn,
And has restored to view its tender green,
That, while the sun rode high, was lost beneath their
   dazzling sheen.
– An emblem this of what the sober Hour
Can do for minds disposed to feel its power!
Thus oft, when we in vain have wish'd away
The petty pleasures of the garish day,
Meek eve shuts up the whole usurping host
(Unbashful dwarfs each glittering at his post)
And leaves the disencumbered spirit free
To reassume a staid simplicity.

   'Tis well – but what are helps of time and place,
When wisdom stands in need of nature's grace;
Why do good thoughts, invoked or not, descend,
Like Angels from their bowers, our virtues to befriend;
If yet To-morrow, unbelied, may say,
'I come to open out, for fresh display,
The elastic vanities of yesterday?'

Desire we past illusions to recal?

Desire we past illusions to recal?
To reinstate wild Fancy, would we hide
Truths whose thick veil Science has drawn aside?
No, – let this Age, high as she may, instal
In her esteem the thirst that wrought man's fall,
The universe is infinitely wide;
And conquering Reason, if self-glorified,
Can nowhere move uncrossed by some new wall
Or gulf of mystery, which thou alone,
Imaginative Faith! canst overleap,
In progress toward the fount of Love, – the throne
Of Power whose ministers the records keep
Of periods fixed, and laws established, less
Flesh to exalt than prove its nothingness.

On Revisiting Dunolly Castle

The captive Bird was gone: – to cliff or moor
Perchance had flown, delivered by the storm;
Or he had pined, and sunk to feed the worm:
Him found we not: but, climbing a tall tower,
There saw, impaved with rude fidelity
Of art mosaic, in a roofless floor,
An Eagle with stretched wings, but beamless eye –
An Eagle that could neither wail nor soar.
Effigy of the Vanished – (shall I dare
To call thee so?) or symbol of fierce deeds
And of the towering courage which past times
Rejoiced in – take, whate'er thou be, a share,
Not undeserved, of the memorial rhymes
That animate my way where'er it leads!

Cave of Staffa

We saw, but surely, in the motley crowd,
Not One of us has felt the far-famed sight;
How *could* we feel it? each the other's blight,
Hurried and hurrying, volatile and loud.
O for those motions only that invite
The Ghost of Fingal to his tuneful Cave
By the breeze entered, and wave after wave
Softly embosoming the timid light!
And by *one* Votary who at will might stand
Gazing and take into his mind and heart,
With undistracted reverence, the effect
Of those proportions where the almighty hand
That made the worlds, the sovereign Architect,
Has deigned to work as if with human Art!

Steamboats, Viaducts, and Railways

Motions and Means, on land and sea at war
With old poetic feeling, not for this,
Shall ye, by Poets even, be judged amiss!
Nor shall your presence, howsoe'er it mar
The loveliness of Nature, prove a bar
To the Mind's gaining that prophetic sense
Of future change, that point of vision, whence
May be discovered what in soul ye are.
In spite of all that beauty may disown
In your harsh features, Nature doth embrace
Her lawful offspring in Man's art; and Time,
Pleased with your triumphs o'er his brother Space,
Accepts from your bold hands the proffered crown
Of hope, and smiles on you with cheer sublime.

Expostulation and Reply

'Why, William, on that old grey stone,
Thus for the length of half a day,
Why, William, sit you thus alone,
And dream your time away?

'Where are your books? – that light bequeathed
To Beings else forlorn and blind!
Up! up! and drink the spirit breathed
From dead men to their kind.

'You look round on your Mother Earth,
As if she for no purpose bore you;
As if you were her first-born birth,
And none had lived before you!'

One morning thus, by Esthwaite lake,
When life was sweet, I knew not why,
To me my good friend Matthew spake,
And thus I made reply:

'The eye – it cannot choose but see;
We cannot bid the ear be still;
Our bodies feel, where'er they be,
Against or with our will.

'Nor less I deem that there are Powers
Which of themselves our minds impress;
That we can feed this mind of ours
In a wise passiveness.

'Think you, 'mid all this mighty sum
Of things for ever speaking,
That nothing of itself will come,
But we must still be seeking?

'– Then ask not wherefore, here, alone,
Conversing as I may,
I sit upon this old grey stone,
And dream my time away.'

The Tables Turned

AN EVENING SCENE ON THE SAME SUBJECT

Up! up! my Friend, and quit your books;
Or surely you'll grow double:
Up! up! my Friend, and clear your looks;
Why all this toil and trouble?

The sun, above the mountain's head,
A freshening lustre mellow
Through all the long green fields has spread,
His first sweet evening yellow.

Books! 'tis a dull and endless strife:
Come, hear the woodland linnet,
How sweet his music! on my life,
There's more of wisdom in it.

And hark! how blithe the throstle sings!
He, too, is no mean preacher:
Come forth into the light of things,
Let Nature be your Teacher.

She has a world of ready wealth,
Our minds and hearts to bless –
Spontaneous wisdom breathed by health,
Truth breathed by cheerfulness.

One impulse from a vernal wood
May teach you more of man,
Of moral evil and of good,
Than all the sages can.

Sweet is the lore which Nature brings;
Our meddling intellect
Mis-shapes the beauteous forms of things: —
We murder to dissect.

Enough of Science and of Art;
Close up those barren leaves;
Come forth, and bring with you a heart
That watches and receives.

A Character

I marvel how Nature could ever find space
For so many strange contrasts in one human face:
There's thought and no thought, and there's paleness and
    bloom
And bustle and sluggishness, pleasure and gloom.

There's weakness, and strength both redundant and vain;
Such strength as, if ever affliction and pain
Could pierce through a temper that's soft to disease,
Would be rational peace – a philosopher's ease.

There's indifference, alike when he fails or succeeds,
And attention full ten times as much as there needs;
Pride where there's no envy, there's so much of joy;
And mildness, and spirit both forward and coy.

There's freedom, and sometimes a diffident stare
Of shame scarcely seeming to know that she's there,
There's virtue, the title it surely may claim,
Yet wants heaven knows what to be worthy the name.

This picture from nature may seem to depart,
Yet the Man would at once run away with your heart;
And I for five centuries right gladly would be
Such an odd such a kind happy creature as he.

A Poet's Epitaph

Art thou a Statist in the van
Of public conflicts trained and bred?
– First learn to love one living man;
Then may'st thou think upon the dead.

A Lawyer art thou? – draw not nigh!
Go, carry to some fitter place
The keenness of that practised eye,
The hardness of that sallow face.

Art thou a Man of purple cheer?
A rosy Man, right plump to see?
Approach; yet, Doctor, not too near,
This grave no cushion is for thee.

Or art thou one of gallant pride,
A Soldier and no man of chaff?
Welcome! – but lay thy sword aside,
And lean upon a peasant's staff.

Physician art thou? – one, all eyes,
Philosopher! – a fingering slave,
One that would peep and botanize
Upon his mother's grave?

Wrapt closely in thy sensual fleece,
O turn aside, – and take, I pray,
That he below may rest in peace,
Thy ever-dwindling soul, away!

A Moralist perchance appears;
Led, Heaven knows how! to this poor sod:
And he has neither eyes nor ears;
Himself his world, and his own God;

One to whose smooth-rubbed soul can cling
Nor form, nor feeling, great or small;
A reasoning, self-sufficing thing,
An intellectual All-in-all!

Shut close the door; press down the latch;
Sleep in thy intellectual crust;
Nor lose ten tickings of thy watch
Near this unprofitable dust.

But who is He, with modest looks,
And clad in homely russet brown?
He murmurs near the running brooks
A music sweeter than their own.

He is retired as noontide dew,
Or fountain in a noon-day grove;
And you must love him, ere to you
He will seem worthy of your love.

The outward shows of sky and earth,
Of hill and valley, he has viewed;
And impulses of deeper birth
Have come to him in solitude.

In common things that round us lie
Some random truths he can impart, –
The harvest of a quiet eye
That broods and sleeps on his own heart.

But he is weak; both Man and Boy,
Hath been an idler in the land;
Contented if he might enjoy
The things which others understand.

– Come hither in thy hour of strength;
Come, weak as is a breaking wave!
Here stretch they body at full length;
Or build thy house upon this grave.

Personal Talk

I

I am not One who much or oft delight
To season my fireside with personal talk, –
Of friends, who live within an easy walk,
Or neighbours, daily, weekly, in my sight:
And, for my chance-acquaintance, ladies bright,
Sons, mothers, maidens withering on the stalk,
These all wear out of me, like Forms, with chalk
Painted on rich men's floors, for one feast-night.
Better than such discourse doth silence long,
Long, barren silence, square with my desire;
To sit without emotion, hope, or aim,
In the loved presence of my cottage-fire,
And listen to the flapping of the flame,
Or kettle whispering its faint undersong.

II

'Yet life,' you say, 'is life; we have seen and see,
And with a living pleasure we describe;
And fits of sprightly malice do but bribe
The languid mind into activity.
Sound sense, and love itself, and mirth and glee
Are fostered by the comment and the gibe.'
Even be it so: yet still among your tribe,
Our daily world's true Worldlings, rank not me!
Children are blest, and powerful; their world lies
More justly balanced; partly at their feet,
And part far from them: – sweetest melodies
Are those that are by distance made more sweet;

Whose mind is but the mind of his own eyes,
He is a Slave; the meanest we can meet!

III

Wings have we, – and as far as we can go
We may find pleasure: wilderness and wood,
Blank ocean and mere sky, support that mood
Which with the lofty sanctifies the low.
Dreams, books, are each a world; and books, we know,
Are a substantial world, both pure and good:
Round these, with tendrils strong as flesh and blood,
Our pastime and our happiness will grow.
There find I personal themes, a plenteous store,
Matter wherein right voluble I am,
To which I listen with a ready ear;
Two shall be named, pre-eminently dear, –
The gentle Lady married to the Moor;
And heavenly Una with her milk-white Lamb.

IV

Nor can I not believe but that hereby
Great gains are mine; for thus I live remote
From evil-speaking; rancour, never sought,
Comes to me not; malignant truth, or lie.
Hence have I genial seasons, hence have I
Smooth passions, smooth discourse, and joyous thought:
And thus from day to day my little boat
Rocks in its harbour, lodging peaceably.
Blessings be with them – and eternal praise,
Who gave us nobler loves, and nobler cares –

The Poets, who on earth have made us heirs
Of truth and pure delight by heavenly lays!
Oh! might my name be numbered among theirs,
Then gladly would I end my mortal days.

Ode to Duty

'Jam non consilio bonus, sed more eò perductus, ut non tantum rectè facere possim, sed nisi rectè facere non possim.'

Stern Daughter of the Voice of God!
O Duty! if that name thou love
Who art a light to guide, a rod
To check the erring, and reprove;
Thou, who art victory and law
When empty terrors overawe;
From vain temptations dost set free;
And calm'st the weary strife of frail humanity!

There are who ask not if thine eye
Be on them; who, in love and truth,
Where no misgiving is, rely
Upon the genial sense of youth;
Glad Hearts! without reproach or blot;
Who do thy work, and know it not:
Oh! if through confidence misplaced
They fail, thy saving arms, dread Power! around them cast.

Serene will be our days and bright,
And happy will our nature be,
When love is an unerring light,
And joy its own security.
And they a blissful course may hold
Even now, who, not unwisely bold,
Live in the spirit of this creed;
Yet seek thy firm support, according to their need.

I, loving freedom, and untried;
No sport of every random gust,
Yet being to myself a guide,
Too blindly have reposed my trust:
And oft, when in my heart was heard
Thy timely mandate, I deferred
The task, in smoother walks to stray;
But thee I now would serve more strictly, if I may.

Through no disturbance of my soul,
Or strong compunction in me wrought,
I supplicate for thy control;
But in the quietness of thought:
Me this unchartered freedom tires;
I feel the weight of chance-desires:
My hopes no more must change their name,
I long for a repose that ever is the same.

[Yet not the less would I throughout
Still act according to the voice
Of my own wish; and feel past doubt
That my submissiveness was choice:
Not seeking in the school of pride
For 'precepts over dignified',
Denial and restraint I prize
No farther than they breed a second Will more wise.]

Stern Lawgiver! yet thou dost wear
The Godhead's most benignant grace;
Nor know we anything so fair
As is the smile upon thy face:
Flowers laugh before thee on their beds
And fragrance in thy footing treads;

Thou dost preserve the stars from wrong;
And the most ancient heavens, through Thee, are fresh
  and strong.

To humbler functions, awful Power!
I call thee: I myself commend
Unto thy guidance from this hour;
Oh, let my weakness have an end!
Give unto me, made lowly wise,
The spirit of self-sacrifice;
The confidence of reason give;
And in the light of truth thy Bondman let me live!

Young England – what is then become of Old

Young England – what is then become of Old
Of dear Old England? Think they she is dead,
Dead to the very name? Presumption fed
On empty air! That name will keep its hold
In the true filial bosom's inmost fold
For ever. – The Spirit of Alfred, at the head
Of all who for her rights watch'd, toil'd and bled,
Knows that this prophecy is not too bold.
What – how! shall she submit in will and deed
To Beardless Boys – an imitative race,
The *servum pecus* of a Gallic breed?
Dear Mother! if thou *must* thy steps retrace,
Go where at least meek Innocency dwells;
Let Babes and Sucklings be thy oracles.

Goody Blake and Harry Gill

A TRUE STORY

Oh! what's the matter? what's the matter?
What is't that ails young Harry Gill?
That evermore his teeth they chatter,
Chatter, chatter, chatter still!
Of waistcoats Harry has no lack,
Good duffle grey, and flannel fine;
He has a blanket on his back,
And coats enough to smother nine.

In March, December, and in July,
'Tis all the same with Harry Gill;
The neighbours tell, and tell you truly,
His teeth they chatter, chatter still.
At night, at morning, and at noon,
'Tis all the same with Harry Gill;
Beneath the sun, beneath the moon,
His teeth they chatter, chatter still!

Young Harry was a lusty drover,
And who so stout of limb as he?
His cheeks were red as ruddy clover;
His voice was like the voice of three.
Old Goody Blake was old and poor;
Ill fed she was, and thinly clad;
And any man who passed her door
Might see how poor a hut she had.

All day she spun in her poor dwelling:
And then her three hours' work at night,
Alas! 'twas hardly worth the telling,
It would not pay for candle-light.

Remote from sheltered village-green,
On a hill's northern side she dwelt,
Where from sea-blasts the hawthorns lean,
And hoary dews are slow to melt.

By the same fire to boil their pottage,
Two poor old Dames, as I have known,
Will often live in one small cottage;
But she, poor Woman! housed alone.
'Twas well enough, when summer came,
The long, warm, lightsome summer-day,
Then at her door the *canty* Dame
Would sit, as any linnet, gay.

But when the ice our streams did fetter,
On then how her old bones would shake!
You would have said, if you had met her,
'Twas a hard time for Goody Blake.
Her evenings then were dull and dead:
Sad case it was, as you may think,
For very cold to go to bed;
And then for cold not sleep a wink.

O joy for her! whene'er in winter
The winds at night had made a rout;
And scattered many a lusty splinter
And many a rotten bough about.
Yet never had she, well or sick,
As every man who knew her says,
A pile beforehand, turf or stick,
Enough to warm her for three days.

Now, when the frost was past enduring,
And made her poor old bones to ache,
Could any thing be more alluring
Than an old hedge to Goody Blake?

And, now and then, it must be said,
When her old bones were cold and chill,
She left her fire, or left her bed,
To seek the hedge of Harry Gill.

Now Harry he had long suspected
This trespass of old Goody Blake;
And vowed that she should be detected –
That he on her would vengeance take.
And oft from his warm fire he'd go,
And to the fields his road would take;
And there, at night, in frost and snow,
He watched to seize old Goody Blake.

And once, behind a rick of barley,
Thus looking out did Harry stand:
The moon was full and shining clearly,
And crisp with frost the stubble land.
– He hears a noise – he's all awake –
Again? – on tip-toe down the hill
He softly creeps – 'tis Goody Blake;
She's at the hedge of Harry Gill!

Right glad was he when he beheld her:
Stick after stick did Goody pull:
He stood behind a bush of elder,
Till she had filled her apron full.
When with her load she turned about,
The by-way back again to take;
He started forward, with a shout,
And sprang upon poor Goody Blake.

And fiercely by the arm he took her,
And by the arm he held her fast,
And fiercely by the arm he shook her,
And cried, 'I've caught you then at last!'

Then Goody, who had nothing said,
Her bundle from her lap let fall;
And, kneeling on the sticks, she prayed
To God that is the judge of all.

She prayed, her withered hand uprearing,
While Harry held her by the arm –
'God! who art never out of hearing,
O may he never more be warm!'
The cold, cold moon above her head,
Thus on her knees did Goody pray;
Young Harry heard what she had said:
And icy cold he turned away.

He went complaining all the morrow
That he was cold and very chill:
His face was gloom, his heart was sorrow,
Alas! that day for Harry Gill!
That day he wore a riding-coat,
But not a whit the warmer he:
Another was on Thursday brought,
And ere the Sabbath he had three.

'Twas all in vain, a useless matter,
And blankets were about him pinned;
Yet still his jaws and teeth they clatter,
Like a loose casement in the wind.
And Harry's flesh it fell away;
And all who see him say, 'tis plain,
That, live as long as live he may,
He never will be warm again.

No word to any man he utters,
A-bed or up, to young or old;
But ever to himself he mutters,
'Poor Harry Gill is very cold.'

A-bed or up, by night or day;
His teeth they chatter, chatter still.
Now think, ye farmers all, I pray,
Of Goody Blake and Harry Gill!

To a Child

WRITTEN IN HER ALBUM

Small service is true service while it lasts:
Of humblest Friends, bright Creature! scorn not one:
The Daisy, by the shadow that it casts,
Protects the lingering dew-drop from the Sun.

Hast thou seen, with flash incessant

Hast thou seen, with flash incessant,
Bubbles gliding under ice,
Bodied forth and evanescent,
No one knows by what device?

Such are thoughts! – A wind-swept meadow
Mimicking a troubled sea,
Such is life; and death a shadow
From the rock eternity!

The Old Cumberland Beggar

The class of Beggars, to which the Old Man here described belongs, will probably soon be extinct. It consisted of poor, and, mostly, old and infirm persons, who confined themselves to a stated round in their neighbourhood, and had certain fixed days, on which, at different houses, they regularly received alms, sometimes in money, but mostly in provisions.

I saw an aged Beggar in my walk;
And he was seated, by the highway side,
On a low structure of rude masonry
Built at the foot of a huge hill, that they
Who lead their horses down the steep rough road
May thence remount at ease. The aged Man
Had placed his staff across the broad smooth stone
That overlays the pile; and, from a bag
All white with flour, the dole of village dames,
He drew his scraps and fragments, one by one;
And scanned them with a fixed and serious look
Of idle computation. In the sun,
Upon the second step of that small pile,
Surrounded by those wild unpeopled hills,
He sat, and ate his food in solitude:
And ever, scattered from his palsied hand,
That, still attempting to prevent the waste,
Was baffled still, the crumbs in little showers
Fell on the ground; and the small mountain birds,
Not venturing yet to peck their destined meal,
Approached within the length of half his staff.

  Him from my childhood have I known; and then
He was so old, he seems not older now;
He travels on, a solitary Man,

So helpless in appearance, that for him
The sauntering Horseman throws not with a slack
And careless hand his alms upon the ground,
But stops, – that he may safely lodge the coin
Within the old Man's hat; nor quits him so,
But still, when he has given his horse the rein,
Watches the aged Beggar with a look
Sidelong, and half-reverted. She who tends
The toll-gate, when in summer at her door
She turns her wheel, if on the road she sees
The aged Beggar coming, quits her work,
And lifts the latch for him that he may pass.
The post-boy, when his rattling wheels o'ertake
The aged Beggar in the woody lane,
Shouts to him from behind; and, if thus warned
The old man does not change his course, the boy
Turns with less noisy wheels to the roadside,
And passes gently by, without a curse
Upon his lips or anger at his heart.

　He travels on, a solitary Man;
His age has no companion. On the ground
His eyes are turned, and, as he moves along,
They move along the ground; and, evermore,
Instead of common and habitual sight
Of fields with rural works, of hill and dale,
And the blue sky, one little span of earth
Is all his prospect. Thus, from day to day.
Bow-bent, his eyes for ever on the ground,
He plies his weary journey; seeing still,
And seldom knowing that he sees, some straw,
Some scattered leaf, or marks which, in one track,
The nails of cart or chariot-wheel have left
Impressed on the white road, – in the same line,

At distance still the same. Poor Traveller!
His staff trails with him: scarcely do his feet
Disturb the summer dust; he is so still
In look and motion, that the cottage curs,
Ere he has passed the door, will turn away,
Weary of barking at him. Boys and girls,
The vacant and the busy, maids and youths,
The urchins newly breeched – all pass him by:
Him even the slow-paced waggon leaves behind.

   But deem not this Man useless – Statesmen! ye
Who are so restless in your wisdom, ye
Who have a broom still ready in your hands
To rid the world of nuisances; ye proud,
Heart-swoln, while in your pride ye contemplate
Your talents, power, or wisdom, deem him not
A burthen of the earth! 'Tis Nature's law
That none, the meanest of created things,
Of forms created the most vile and brute,
The dullest or most noxious, should exist
Divorced from good – a spirit and pulse of good,
A life and soul, to every mode of being
Inseparably linked. Then be assured
That least of all can aught – that ever owned
The heaven-regarding eye and front sublime
Which man is born to – sink, howe'er depressed,
So low as to be scorned without a sin;
Without offence to God cast out of view;
Like the dry remnant of a garden-flower
Whose seeds are shed, or as an implement
Worn out and worthless. While from door to door,
This old Man creeps, the villagers in him
Behold a record which together binds
Past deeds and offices of charity

Else unremembered, and so keeps alive
The kindly mood in hearts which lapse of years,
And that half-wisdom half-experience gives,
Make slow to feel, and by sure steps resign
To selfishness and cold oblivious cares.
Among the farms and solitary huts,
Hamlets and thinly-scattered villages,
Where'er the aged Beggar takes his rounds,
The mild necessity of use compels
To acts of love; and habit does the work
Of reason; yet prepares that after-joy
Which reason cherishes. And thus the soul,
By that sweet taste of pleasure unpursued,
Doth find herself insensibly disposed
To virtue and true goodness. Some there are,
By their good works exalted, lofty minds,
And meditative, authors of delight
And happiness, which to the end of time
Will live, and spread, and kindle: even such minds
In childhood, from this solitary Being,
Or from like wanderer, haply have received
(A thing more precious far than all that books
Or the solicitudes of love can do!)
That first mild touch of sympathy and thought,
In which they found their kindred with a world
Where want and sorrow were. The easy man
Who sits at his own door, – and, like the pear
That overhangs his head from the green wall,
Feeds in the sunshine; the robust and young,
The prosperous and unthinking, they who live
Sheltered, and flourish in a little grove
Of their own kindred; – all behold in him
A silent monitor, which on their minds
Must needs impress a transitory thought

Of self-congratulation, to the heart
Of each recalling his peculiar boons,
His charters and exemptions; and, perchance,
Though he to no one give the fortitude
And circumspection needful to preserve
His present blessings, and to husband up
The respite of the season, he, at least,
And 'tis no vulgar service, makes them felt.

   Yet further. — Many, I believe, there are
Who live a life of virtuous decency,
Men who can hear the Decalogue and feel
No self-reproach; who of the moral law
Established in the land where they abide
Are strict observers; and not negligent
In acts of love to those with whom they dwell,
Their kindred, and the children of their blood.
Praise be to such, and to their slumbers peace!
– But of the poor man ask, the abject poor;
Go, and demand of him, if there be here
In this cold abstinence from evil deeds,
And these inevitable charities,
Wherewith to satisfy the human soul?

No – Man is dear to man; the poorest poor
Long for some moments in a weary life
When they can know and feel that they have been,
Themselves, the fathers and the dealers-out
Of some small blessings; have been kind to such
As needed kindness, for this single cause,
That we have all of us one human heart.
– Such pleasure is to one kind Being known,
My neighbour, when with punctual care, each week,
Duly as Friday comes, though pressed herself

By her own wants, she from her store of meal
Takes one unsparing handful for the scrip
Of this old Mendicant, and, from her door
Returning with exhilarated heart,
Sits by her fire, and builds her hope in heaven.

Then let him pass, a blessing on his head!
And while in that vast solitude to which
The tide of things has borne him, he appears
To breathe and live but for himself alone,
Unblamed, uninjured, let him bear about
The good which the benignant law of Heaven
Has hung around him: and, while life is his,
Still let him prompt the unlettered villagers
To tender offices and pensive thoughts.
– Then let him pass, a blessing on his head!
And, long as he can wander, let him breathe
The freshness of the valleys; let his blood
Struggle with frosty air and winter snows;
And let the chartered wind that sweeps the heath
Beat his grey locks against his withered face.
Reverence the hope whose vital anxiousness
Gives the last human interest to his heart.
May never HOUSE, misnamed of INDUSTRY,
Make him a captive! – for that pent-up din,
Those life-consuming sounds that clog the air,
Be his the natural silence of old age!
Let him be free of mountain solitudes;
And have around him, whether heard or not,
The pleasant melody of woodland birds.
Few are his pleasures: if his eyes have now
Been doomed so long to settle upon earth
That not without some effort they behold
The countenance of the horizontal sun,

Rising or setting, let the light at least
Find a free entrance to their languid orbs,
And let him, *where* and *when* he will, sit down
Beneath the trees, or on a grassy bank
Of highway side, and with the little birds
Share his chance-gathered meal; and, finally,
As in the eye of Nature he has lived,
So in the eye of Nature let him die!

Animal Tranquillity and Decay

The little hedgerow birds,
That peck along the road, regard him not.
He travels on, and in his face, his step,
His gait, is one expression: every limb,
His look and bending figure, all bespeak
A man who does not move with pain, but moves
With thought. – He is insensibly subdued
To settled quiet: he is one by whom
All effort seems forgotten; one to whom
Long patience hath such mild composure given,
That patience now doth seem a thing of which
He hath no need. He is by nature led
To peace so perfect that the young behold
With envy, what the Old Man hardly feels.

Invocation to the Earth

February, 1816

I

     'REST, rest, perturbed Earth!
     O rest, thou doleful Mother of Mankind!'
A Spirit sang in tones more plaintive than the wind:
'From regions where no evil thing has birth
I come – thy stains to wash away,
Thy cherished fetters to unbind,
And open thy sad eyes upon a milder day.
The Heavens are thronged with martyrs that have risen
    From out thy noisome prison;
    The penal caverns groan
With tens of thousands rent from off the tree
Of hopeful life, – by battle's whirlwind blown
Into the deserts of Eternity.
Unpitied havoc! Victims unlamented!
But not on high, where madness is resented,
And murder causes some sad tears to flow,
Though, from the widely-sweeping blow,
The choirs of Angels spread, triumphantly augmented.

II

     'False Parent of Mankind!
     Obdurate, proud, and blind,
I sprinkle thee with soft celestial dews,
Thy lost, maternal heart to re-infuse!
Scattering this far-fetched moisture from my wings,
Upon the act a blessing I implore,
Of which the rivers in their secret springs,

The rivers stained so oft with human gore,
Are conscious; – may the like return no more!
May Discord – for a Seraph's care
Shall be attended with a bolder prayer –
May she, who once disturbed the seats of bliss
       These mortal spheres above,
Be chained for ever to the black abyss!
And thou, O rescued Earth, by peace and love,
And merciful desires, thy sanctity approve!'
  The Spirit ended his mysterious rite,
And the pure vision closed in darkness infinite.

Ode

INTIMATIONS OF IMMORTALITY FROM
RECOLLECTIONS OF EARLY CHILDHOOD

>   The Child is father of the Man;
>   And I could wish my days to be
>   Bound each to each by natural piety.

I

There was a time when meadow, grove, and stream,
The earth, and every common sight,
            To me did seem
            Apparelled in celestial light,
The glory and the freshness of a dream.
It is not now as it hath been of yore; –
            Turn wheresoe'er I may,
            By night or day,
The things which I have seen I now can see no more.

II

            The Rainbow comes and goes,
            And lovely is the Rose,
            The Moon doth with delight
Look round her when the heavens are bare;
            Waters on a starry night
            Are beautiful and fair;
    The sunshine is a glorious birth;
    But yet I know, where'er I go,
    That there hath past away a glory from the earth.

III

Now, while the birds thus sing a joyous song,
  And while the young lambs bound
    As to the tabor's sound,
To me alone there came a thought of grief:
A timely utterance gave that thought relief,
    And I again am strong:
The cataracts blow their trumpets from the steep;
No more shall grief of mine the season wrong;
I hear the Echoes through the mountains throng,
The Winds come to me from the fields of sleep,
      And all the earth is gay;
        Land and sea
      Give themselves up to jollity,
        And with the heart of May
      Doth every Beast keep holiday; –
        Thou Child of Joy,
Shout round me, let me hear thy shouts, thou happy
  Shepherd-boy!

IV

Ye blessèd Creatures, I have heard the call
  Ye to each other make; I see
The heavens laugh with you in your jubilee;
  My heart is at your festival,
    My head hath its coronal,
The fulness of your bliss, I feel – I feel it all.
      Oh evil day! if I were sullen
      While Earth herself is adorning,
        This sweet May-morning,
      And the Children are culling
        On every side,
      In a thousand valleys far and wide,

Fresh flowers; while the sun shines warm,
And the Babe leaps up on his Mother's arm: –
I hear, I hear, with joy I hear!
– But there's a Tree, of many, one,
A single Field which I have looked upon,
Both of them speak of something that is gone:
The Pansy at my feet
Doth the same tale repeat:
Whither is fled the visionary gleam?
Where is it now, the glory and the dream?

v

Our birth is but a sleep and a forgetting:
The Soul that rises with us, our life's Star,
Hath had elsewhere its setting,
And cometh from afar:
Not in entire forgetfulness,
And not in utter nakedness,
But trailing clouds of glory do we come
From God, who is our home:
Heaven lies about us in our infancy!
Shades of the prison-house begin to close
Upon the growing Boy,
But He
Beholds the light, and whence it flows,
He sees it in his joy;
The Youth, who daily farther from the east
Must travel, still is Nature's Priest,
And by the vision splendid
Is on his way attended;
At length the Man perceives it die away,
And fade into the light of common day.

VI

Earth fills her lap with pleasures of her own;
Yearnings she hath in her own natural kind,
And, even with something of a Mother's mind,
          And no unworthy aim,
          The homely Nurse doth all she can
To make her Foster-child, her Inmate Man,
          Forget the glories he hath known,
And that imperial palace whence he came.

VII

Behold the Child among his new-born blisses,
A six years' Darling of a pigmy size!
See, where 'mid work of his own hand he lies,
Frettied by sallies of his mother's kisses,
With light upon him from his father's eyes!
See, at his feet, some little plan or chart,
Some fragment from his dream of human life,
Shaped by himself with newly-learned art;
          A wedding or a festival,
          A mourning or a funeral;
              And this hath now his heart,
          And unto this he frames his song:
              Then will he fit his tongue
To dialogues of business, love, or strife;
          But it will not be long
          Ere this be thrown aside,
          And with new joy and pride
The little Actor cons another part;
Filling from time to time his 'humorous stage'
With all the Persons, down to palsied Age,
That Life brings with her in her equipage;
          As if his whole vocation
          Were endless imitation.

VIII

Thou, whose exterior semblance doth belie
     Thy Soul's immensity;
Thou best Philosopher, who yet dost keep
Thy heritage, thou Eye among the blind,
That, deaf and silent, read'st the eternal deep,
Haunted for ever by the eternal mind, –
     Mighty Prophet! Seer blest!
     On whom those truths do rest,
Which we are toiling all our lives to find,
In darkness lost, the darkness of the grave;
Thou, over whom thy Immortality
Broods like the Day, a Master o'er a Slave,
A Presence which is not to be put by;
Thou little Child, yet glorious in the might
Of heaven-born freedom on thy being's height,
Why with such earnest pains dost thou provoke
The years to bring the inevitable yoke,
Thus blindly with thy blessedness at strife?
Full soon thy Soul shall have her earthly freight,
And custom lie upon thee with a weight,
Heavy as frost, and deep almost as life!

IX

     O joy! that in our embers
     Is something that doth live,
     That nature yet remembers
     What was so fugitive!
The thought of our past years in me doth breed
Perpetual benediction: not indeed
For that which is most worthy to be blest;
Delight and liberty, the simple creed
Of Childhood, whether busy or at rest,

With new-fledged hope still fluttering in his breast: –
  Not for these I raise
  The song of thanks and praise;
 But for those obstinate questionings
 Of sense and outward things,
 Fallings from us, vanishings;
 Blank misgivings of a Creature
Moving about in worlds not realised,
High instincts before which our mortal Nature
Did tremble like a guilty Thing surprised:
  But for those first affections,
  Those shadowy recollections,
  Which, be they what they may,
Are yet the fountain light of all our day,
Are yet a master light of all our seeing;
  Uphold us, cherish, and have power to make
Our noisy years seem moments in the being
Of the eternal Silence: truths that wake,
  To perish never;
Which neither listlessness, nor mad endeavour,
  Nor Man nor Boy,
Nor all that is at enmity with joy,
Can utterly abolish or destroy!
  Hence in a season of calm weather
  Though inland far we be,
Our Souls have sight of that immortal sea
  Which brought us hither,
  Can in a moment travel thither,
And see the Children sport upon the shore,
And hear the mighty waters rolling evermore.

X

Then sing, ye Birds, sing, sing a joyous song!
  And let the young Lambs bound

   As to the tabor's sound!
We in thought will join your throng,
   Ye that pipe and ye that play,
   Ye that through your hearts to-day
   Feel the gladness of the May!
What though the radiance which was once so bright
Be now for ever taken from my sight,
   Though nothing can bring back the hour
Of splendour in the grass, of glory in the flower;
   We will grieve not, rather find
   Strength in what remains behind;
   In the primal sympathy
   Which having been must ever be;
   In the soothing thoughts that spring
   Out of human suffering;
   In the faith that looks through death,
In years that bring the philosophic mind.

XI

And O, ye Fountains, Meadows, Hills, and Groves,
Forebode not any severing of our loves!
Yet in my heart of hearts I feel your might;
I only have relinquished one delight
To live beneath your more habitual sway.
I love the Brooks which down their channels fret,
Even more than when I tripped lightly as they;
The innocent brightness of a new-born Day
   Is lovely yet;
The Clouds that gather round the setting sun
Do take a sober colouring from an eye
That hath kept watch o'er man's mortality;
Another race hath been, and other palms are won.

Thanks to the human heart by which we live,
Thanks to its tenderness, its joys, and fears,
To me the meanest flower that blows can give
Thoughts that do often lie too deep for tears.

From the Alfoxden Notebook

Away, away, it is the air
That stirs among the wither'd leaves;
Away, away, it is not there,
Go, hunt among the harvest sheaves.
There is a bed in shape as plain
As from a hare or lion's lair
It is the bed where we have lain
In anguish and despair.

Away, and take the eagle's eye,
The tyger's smell,
Ears that can hear the agonies
And murmurings of hell;
And when you there have stood
By that same bed of pain,
The groans are gone, the tears remain.
Then tell me if the thing be clear,
The difference betwixt a tear
Of water and of blood.

Written in the Strangers' Book at 'The Station', opposite Bowness

My Lord and Lady Darlington,
I would not speak in snarling tone;
Nor to you, good Lady Vane,
Would I give a moment's pain;
Nor Miss Taylor, Captain Stamp,
Would I your flights of *memory* cramp.
Yet, having spent a summer's day
On the green margin of Loch Tay,
And doubled (prospect ever bettering)
The mazy reaches of Loch Katerine,
And more than once been free at Luss,
Loch Lomond's beauties to discuss,
And wished, at least, to hear the blarney
Of the sly boatmen of Killarney,
And dipped my hand in dancing wave
Of Eau de Zurich, Lac Genève,
And bowed to many a major-domo
On stately terraces of Como,
And seen the Simplon's forehead hoary,
Reclined on Lago Maggiore,
At breathless eventide at rest
On the broad water's placid breast, –
I, not insensible, Heaven knows,
To all the charms this Station shows,
Must tell you, Captain, Lord and Ladies,
For honest worth one poet's trade is,
That your praise appears to me
Folly's own hyperbole.

from The Prelude (*1850 edition*)

from BOOK I: CHILDHOOD AND SCHOOL-TIME

... One summer evening (led by her) I found
A little boat tied to a willow tree
Within a rocky cave, its usual home.
Straight I unloosed her chain, and stepping in
Pushed from the shore. It was an act of stealth
And troubled pleasure, nor without the voice
Of mountain-echoes did my boat move on;
Leaving behind her still, on either side,
Small circles glittering idly in the moon,
Until they melted all into one track
Of sparkling light. But now, like one who rows,
Proud of his skill, to reach a chosen point
With an unswerving line, I fixed my view
Upon the summit of a craggy ridge,
The horizon's utmost boundary, for above
Was nothing but the stars and the grey sky.
She was an elfin pinnace; lustily
I dipped my oars into the silent lake,
And, as I rose upon the stroke, my boat
Went heaving through the water like a swan;
When, from behind that craggy steep till then
The horizon's bound, a huge peak, black and huge,
As if with voluntary power instinct
Upreared its head. I struck and struck again,
And growing still in stature the grim shape
Towered up between me and the stars, and still,
For so it seemed, with purpose of its own
And measured motion like a living thing,
Strode after me. With trembling oars I turned,

And through the silent water stole my way
Back to the covert of the willow tree;
There in her mooring-place I left my bark, –
And through the meadows homeward went, in grave
And serious mood; but after I had seen
That spectacle, for many days, my brain
Worked with a dim and undetermined sense
Of unknown modes of being; o'er my thoughts
There hung a darkness, call it solitude
Or blank desertion. No familiar shapes
Remained, no pleasant images of trees,
Of sea or sky, no colours of green fields;
But huge and mighty forms, that do not live
Like living men, moved slowly through the mind
By day, and were a trouble to my dreams.

    Wisdom and Spirit of the universe!
Thou Soul that art the eternity of thought,
That giv'st to forms and images a breath
And everlasting motion, not in vain
By day or star-light thus from my first dawn
Of childhood didst thou intertwine for me
The passions that build up our human soul;
Not with the mean and vulgar works of man,
But with high objects, with enduring things –
With life and Nature, purifying thus
The elements of feeling and of thought,
And sanctifying, by such discipline,
Both pain and fear, until we recognize
A grandeur in the beatings of the heart.
Nor was this fellowship vouchsafed to me
With stinted kindness. In November days,
When vapours rolling down the valley made
A lonely scene more lonesome, among woods

At noon, and 'mid the calm of summer nights,
When, by the margin of the trembling lake,
Beneath the gloomy hills homeward I went
In solitude, such intercourse was mine;
Mine was it in the fields both day and night,
And by the waters, all the summer long.

   And in the frosty season, when the sun
Was set, and visible for many a mile
The cottage windows blazed through twilight gloom,
I heeded not their summons: happy time
It was indeed for all of us – for me
It was a time of rapture! Clear and loud
The village clock tolled six, – I wheeled about,
Proud and exulting like an untired horse
That cares not for his home. All shod with steel,
We hissed along the polished ice in games
Confederate, imitative of the chase
And woodland pleasures, – the resounding horn,
The pack loud chiming, and the hunted hare.
So through the darkness and the cold we flew,
And not a voice was idle; with the din
Smitten, the precipices rang aloud;
The leafless trees and every icy crag
Tinkled like iron; while far distant hills
Into the tumult sent an alien sound
Of melancholy not unnoticed, while the stars
Eastward were sparkling clear, and in the west
The orange sky of evening died away.
Not seldom from the uproar I retired
Into a silent bay, or sportively
Glanced sideway, leaving the tumultuous throng,
To cut across the reflex of a star
That fled, and, flying still before me, gleamed

Upon the glassy plain; and oftentimes,
When we had given our bodies to the wind,
And all the shadowy banks on either side
Came sweeping through the darkness, spinning still
The rapid line of motion, then at once
Have I, reclining back upon my heels,
Stopped short; yet still the solitary cliffs
Wheeled by me – even as if the earth had rolled
With visible motion her diurnal round!
Behind me did they stretch in solemn train,
Feebler and feebler, and I stood and watched
Till all was tranquil as a dreamless sleep.

  Ye Presences of Nature in the sky
And on the earth! Ye Visions of the hills!
And Souls of lonely places! can I think
A vulgar hope was yours when ye employed
Such ministry, when ye through many a year
Haunting me thus among my boyish sports,
On caves and trees, upon the woods and hills,
Impressed upon all forms the characters
Of danger or desire; and thus did make
The surface of the universal earth
With triumph and delight, with hope and fear,
Work like a sea?
                    Not uselessly employed,
Might I pursue this theme through every change
Of exercise and play, to which the year
Did summon us in his delightful round ...

from BOOK XI : FRANCE

... O pleasant exercise of hope and joy!
For mighty were the auxiliars which then stood
Upon our side, we who were strong in love!
Bliss was it in that dawn to be alive,
But to be young was very Heaven! O times,
In which the meagre, stale, forbidding ways
Of custom, law, and statute, took at once
The attraction of a country in romance!
When Reason seemed the most to assert her rights
When most intent on making of herself
A prime enchantress to assist the work,
Which then was going forward in her name!
Not favoured spots alone, but the whole Earth,
The beauty wore of promise – that which sets
(As at some moments might not be unfelt
Among the bowers of Paradise itself)
The budding rose above the rose full blown.
What temper at the prospect did not wake
To happiness unthought of? The inert
Were roused, and lively natures rapt away!
They who had fed their childhood upon dreams,
The play-fellows of fancy, who had made
All powers of swiftness, subtlety, and strength
Their ministers, – who in lordly wise had stirred
Among the grandest objects of the sense,
And dealt with whatsoever they found there
As if they had within some lurking right
To wield it; – they, too, who of gentle mood
Had watched all gentle motions, and to these
Had fitted their own thoughts, schemers more mild,
And in the region of their peaceful selves; –

Now was it that *both* found, the meek and lofty
Did both find, helpers to their hearts' desire,
And stuff at hand, plastic as they could wish, –
Were called upon to exercise their skill,
Not in Utopia, – subterranean fields, –
Or some secreted island, Heaven knows where!
But in the very world, which is the world
Of all of us, – the place where, in the end,
We find our happiness, or not at all! ...

... But now, become oppressors in their turn,
Frenchmen had changed a war of self-defence
For one of conquest, losing sight of all
Which they had struggled for: up mounted now,
Openly in the eye of earth and heaven,
The scale of liberty. I read her doom,
With anger vexed, with disappointment sore,
But not dismayed, nor taking to the shame
Of a false prophet. While resentment rose
Striving to hide, what nought could heal, the wounds
Of mortified presumption, I adhered
More firmly to old tenets, and, to prove
Their temper, strained them more; and thus, in heat
Of contest, did opinions every day
Grow into consequence, till round my mind
They clung, as if they were its life, nay more,
The very being of the immortal soul.

   This was the time, when, all things tending fast
To deprivation, speculative schemes –
That promised to abstract the hopes of Man
Out of his feelings, to be fixed thenceforth
For ever in a purer element –
Found ready welcome. Tempting region *that*

For Zeal to enter and refresh herself,
Where passions had the privilege to work,
And never hear the sound of their own names.
But, speaking more in charity, the dream
Flattered the young, pleased with extremes, nor least
With that which makes our Reason's naked self
The object of its fervour. What delight!
How glorious! in self-knowledge and self-rule,
To look through all the frailties of the world,
And, with a resolute mastery shaking off
Infirmities of nature, time, and place,
Build social upon personal Liberty,
Which, to the blind restraints of general laws
Superior, magisterially adopts
One guide, the light of circumstances, flashed
Upon an independent intellect.
Thus expectation rose again; thus hope,
From her first ground expelled, grew proud once more.
Oft, as my thoughts were turned to human kind,
I scorned indifference; but, inflamed with thirst
Of a secure intelligence, and sick
Of other longing, I pursued what seemed
A more exalted nature; wished that Man
Should start out of his earthy, worm-like state,
And spread abroad the wings of Liberty,
Lord of himself, in undisturbed delight –
A noble aspiration! *yet* I feel
(Sustained by worthier as by wiser thoughts)
The aspiration, nor shall ever cease
To feel it; – but return we to our course.

from The Excursion

from BOOK I: THE WANDERER

... Ocean and earth, the solid frame of earth
And ocean's liquid mass, in gladness lay
Beneath him: – Far and wide the clouds were touched,
And in their silent faces could he read
Unutterable love. Sound needed none,
Nor any voice of joy: his spirit drank
The spectacle: sensation, soul, and form,
All melted into him; they swallowed up
His animal being; in them did he live,
And by them did he live; they were his life.
In such access of mind, in such high hour
Of visitation from the living God,
Thought was not; in enjoyment it expired.
No thanks he breathed, he proffered no request;
Rapt into still communion that transcends
The imperfect offices of prayer and praise,
His mind was a thanksgiving to the power
That made him; it was blessedness and love!

A Herdsman on the lonely mountain-tops,
Such intercourse was his, and in this sort
Was his existence oftentimes *possessed*.
O then how beautiful, how bright, appeared
The written promise! Early had he learned
To reverence the volume that displays
The mystery, the life which cannot die;
But in the mountains did he *feel* his faith ...

from BOOK V : THE PASTOR

... 'High on the breast of yon dark mountain, dark
With stony barrenness, a shining speck
Bright as a sunbeam sleeping till a shower
Brush it away, or cloud pass over it;
And such it might be deemed – a sleeping sunbeam;
But 'tis a plot of cultivated ground,
Cut off, an island in the dusky waste;
And that attractive brightness is its own.
The lofty site, by nature framed to tempt
Amid a wilderness of rocks and stones
The tiller's hand, a hermit might have chosen,
For opportunity presented, thence
Far forth to send his wandering eye o'er land
And ocean, and look down upon the works,
The habitations, and the ways of men,
Himself unseen! But no tradition tells
That ever hermit dipped his maple dish
In the sweet spring that lurks 'mid yon green fields;
And no such visionary views belong
To those who occupy and till the ground,
High on that mountain where they long have dwelt
A wedded pair in childless solitude ...

... There, or within the compass of her fields,
At any moment may the Dame be found,
True as the stock-dove to her shallow nest
And to the grove that holds it. She beguiles
By intermingled work of house and field
The summer's day, and winter's; with success
Not equal, but sufficient to maintain,
Even at the worst, a smooth stream of content,

Until the expected hour at which her Mate
From the far-distant quarry's vault returns;
And by his converse crowns a silent day
With evening cheerfulness. In powers of mind,
In scale of culture, few among my flock
Hold lower rank than this sequestered pair:
But true humility descends from heaven;
And that best gift of heaven hath fallen on them;
Abundant recompense for every want.
– Stoop from your height, ye proud, and copy these!
Who, in their noiseless dwelling-place, can hear
The voice of wisdom whispering scripture texts
For the mind's government, or temper's peace;
And recommending for their mutual need,
Forgiveness, patience, hope, and charity!' ...

from BOOK VI: THE CHURCHYARD
AMONG THE MOUNTAINS

... 'Close to his destined habitation, lies
One who achieved a humbler victory,
Though marvellous in its kind. A place there is
High in these mountains, that allured a band
Of keen adventurers to unite their pains
In search of precious ore: they tried, were foiled –
And all desisted, all, save him alone.
He, taking counsel of his own clear thoughts,
And trusting only to his own weak hands,
Urged unremittingly the stubborn work,
Unseconded, uncountenanced; then, as time
Passed on, while still his lonely efforts found
No recompense, derided; and at length,
By many pitied, as insane of mind;

By others dreaded as the luckless thrall
Of subterranean Spirits feeding hope
By various mockery of sight and sound;
Hope after hope, encouraged and destroyed.
– But when the lord of seasons had matured
The fruits of earth through space of twice ten years,
The mountain's entrails offered to his view
And trembling grasp the long-deferred reward.
Not with more transport did Columbus greet
A world, his rich discovery! But our Swain,
A very hero till his point was gained,
Proved all unable to support the weight
Of prosperous fortune. On the fields he looked
With an unsettled liberty of thought,
Wishes and endless schemes; by daylight walked
Giddy and restless; ever and anon
Quaffed in his gratitude immoderate cups;
And truly might be said to die of joy!
He vanished; but conspicuous to this day
The path remains that linked his cottage-door
To the mine's mouth; a long and slanting track,
Upon the rugged mountain's stony side,
Worn by his daily visits to and from
The darksome centre of a constant hope.
This vestige, neither force of beating rain,
Nor the vicissitudes of frost and thaw
Shall cause to fade, till ages pass away;
And it is named, in memory of the event,
The PATH OF PERSEVERANCE.'

                                   'Thou from whom
Man has his strength,' exlaimed the Wanderer, 'oh!
Do thou direct it! To the virtuous grant
The penetrative eye which can perceive

In this blind world the guiding vein of hope;
That, like this Labourer, such may dig their way,
"Unshaken, unseduced, unterrified;"
Grant to the wise *his* firmness of resolve!' . . .

Penguin English Poets

William Wordsworth: The Prelude
A Parallel Text

Edited by J. C. Maxwell

Wordsworth's great autobiographical poem, subtitled *Growth of a Poet's Mind*, was completed in 1805–6. During the rest of his life his interest in the work persisted, and the poem was several times revised, to be published soon after his death in 1850. Originally intended as the first part of a massive three-part poem, *The Prelude* contains some of the greatest poetry Wordsworth wrote on those events and feelings of his youth which lie behind so much of his most powerful work.

Critics and readers have differed over the relative merits of the 1805–6 and 1850 versions of the poem. The two versions are here presented in parallel for the first time in a paperback edition, and the edition has been so designed as to enable the reader to follow either version without interruption, or to compare the versions should he so wish. The manuscripts have been re-examined and many errors in both texts corrected from manuscript evidence. The editor's introduction and notes comment on the manuscript history of the poem and deal with points of difficulty.

Also available

Robert Browning: The Ring and the Book
Edited by Richard D. Altick

Lord Byron: Don Juan
Edited by T. G. Steffan, W. W. Pratt and E. Steffan

John Donne: The Complete English Poems
Edited by A. J. Smith

Samuel Johnson: The Complete English Poems
Edited by J. D. Fleeman

Christopher Marlowe: The Complete Poems and Translations
Edited by Stephen Orgel

Sir Gawain and the Green Knight
Edited by J. A. Burrow

Penguin Education Books

Penguin Modern Poets

1* Lawrence Durrell   Elizabeth Jennings   R. S. Thomas
2* Kingsley Amis   Dom Moraes   Peter Porter
3* George Barker   Martin Bell   Charles Causley
4* David Holbrook   Christopher Middleton   David Wevill
5† Gregory Corso   Lawrence Ferlinghett i   Allen Ginsberg
6   George MacBeth   Edward Lucie-Smith   Jack Clemo
7* Richard Murphy   Jon Silkin   Nathaniel Tarn
8* Edwin Brock   Geoffrey Hill   Stevie Smith
9† Denise Levertov   Kenneth Rexroth   William Carlos Williams
10   Adrian Henri   Roger McGough   Brian Patten
11   D. M. Black   Peter Redgrove   D .M . Thomas
12* Alan Jackson   Jeff Nuttall   William Wantling
13   Charles Bukowski   Philip Lamantia   Harold Norse
14   Alan Brownjohn   Michael Hamburger   Charles Tomlinson
15   Alan Bold   Edward Brathwaite   Edwin Morgan
16   Jack Beeching   Harry Guest   Matthew Mead
17   W. S. Graham   Kathleen Raine   David Gascoyne
18   A. Alvarez   Roy Fuller   Anthony Thwaite
19   John Ashbery   Lee Harwood   Tom Raworth
20   John Heath-Stubbs   F. T. Prince   Stephen Spender
21* George Mackay Brown   Norman MacCaig   Iain Crichton Smith
22* John Fuller   Peter Levi   Adrian Mitchell
23   Geoffrey Grigson   Edwin Muir   Adrian Stokes

* Not for sale in the U.S.A.
† Not for sale in the U.S.A. or Canada

Penguin Modern European Poets

This series now includes selected work by the following poets,
in verse translations by, among others, W. H. Auden, Lawrence
Ferlinghetti, Michael Hamburger, Ted Hughes, J. B. Leishman,
Christopher Middleton and David Wevill:

Amichai

Apollinaire

Bobrowski/Bienek

Celan

Ekelöf

Enzensberger

Four Greek Poets:
Cavafy/Elytis/Gatsos/Seferis

Grass

Guillevic

Haavikko/Tranströmer

Holan

Holub

Kovner/Sachs

Montale

Pavese

Pessoa

Popa

Quasimodo

Rilke

Three Czech Poets:
Nezval/Bartušek/Hanzlík

Tsvetayeva

Ungaretti

Weöres/Juhász

Yevtushenko

Poem into Poem

World Poetry in Modern Verse Translation

Edited by George Steiner

Poem into Poem is the first book of its kind. In an anthology of verse translations from twenty-two languages (ranging from ancient Hebrew and Greek to modern Chinese), each one has been made by an English or American poet who not only renders the original but also creates what is a living poem in its own right.

We find extraordinary encounters – Hardy and Sappho, Hopkins and Horace, Yeats and Ronsard, Scott Fitzgerald and Rimbaud, James Joyce and Gottfried Keller, Ezra Pound and Sophocles. The light of another poem is caught in a live mirror.

George Steiner believes that translation is central to the nature of modern poetry; that ours is the most brilliant period of poetic translation and recapture since the Elizabethans. This anthology contains his evidence.

Not for sale in the U.S.A. or Canada

Poet to Poet

In the introductions to their personal selections from the work of poets they have admired, the individual editors write as follows:

Crabbe Selected by C. Day Lewis

'As his poetry displays a balance and decorum in its versification, so his moral ideal is a kind of normality to which every civilized being should aspire. This, when one looks at the desperate expedients and experiments of poets (and others) today, is at least refreshing.'

Henryson Selected by Hugh MacDiarmid

'There is now a consensus of judgement that regards Henryson as the greatest of our great makars. Literary historians and other commentators in the bad period of the century preceding the twenties of our own century were wont to group together as the great five: Henryson, Dunbar, Douglas, Lyndsay, and King James I; but in the critical atmosphere prevailing today it is clear that Henryson (who was, with the exception of King James, the youngest of them) is the greatest.'

Herbert Selected by W. H. Auden

'The two English poets, neither of them, perhaps, major poets, whom I would most like to have known well, are William Barnes and George Herbert.

'Even if Isaac Walton had never written his life, I think that any reader of his poetry will conclude that George Herbert must have been an exceptionally good man, and exceptionally nice as well.'

Poet to Poet

Whitman Selected by Robert Creeley

'If Whitman has taught me anything, and he has taught me a great deal, often against my own will, it is that the common *is* personal, intensely so, in that having no-one thus to invest it, the sea becomes a curious mixture of water and table salt and the sky the chemical formula for air. It is, paradoxically, the personal which makes the common in so far as recognizes the existence of the many in the one. In my own joy or despair, I am brought to that which others have also experienced.'

Tennyson Selected by Kingsley Amis

'England notoriously had its doubts as well as its certainties, its neuroses as well as its moral health, its fits of gloom and frustration and panic as well as its complacency. Tennyson is the voice of those doubts and their accompaniments, and his genius enabled him to communicate them in such a way that we can understand them and feel them as our own. In short we know from experience just what he means. Eliot called him the saddest of all English poets, and I cannot improve on that judgement.'